ALE

CU00858403

Murder on the Occident Express

Penny Küfer investigates

A gripping murder mystery from the heart of Europe

Cover design: Estella Vukovic
Editor: Tarryn Thomas

www.alexwagner.at

1

Austria, Vienna Central Station
December 9, 6:40 pm

"Penny Küfer," the young woman with the fiery red curls introduced herself. Her real name was Penelope, but she hated the sound of it. Which mother in modern times would punish her child with such a name?

Penny knew the answer, had been living with it for twenty-nine years now: a woman who was herself called Frederike, and who could easily have made it into the *Guinness Book of World Records* in terms of stuffiness and narrow-mindedness.

The steward, the logo of the Occident Express emblazoned on his immaculate uniform, didn't need to consult a guest list. He seemed to have the names of all the evening's passengers committed to memory; which was less surprising than it might sound, since the Occident Express was the most exclusive of all trains currently frequenting the rails of Europe. It boasted just twelve guest compartments, each as spacious and luxurious as a suite in a five-star hotel.

The steward put on a professional smile, bowed slightly and said, "Welcome aboard, Ms. Küfer." Then he took a step to one side and let Penny walk across the red carpet leading to the train.

The platform at Vienna Central Station, from which

the Occident Express would depart in twenty minutes, had been closed to the general public. Only the guests of the luxury train were allowed to walk across the deep pile carpet, at the head of which the receptionist stood guard.

A luggage cart appeared behind the man and, as if steered by an invisible hand, pulled up to Penny and came to a stop exactly next to her suitcase. It was a self-driving vehicle, gleaming with a sleek design.

The steward bent down and lifted Penny's luggage onto the cart. When he noticed her astonished look, he smiled. "With us, everything is high-tech," he explained, with unmistakable pride in his voice.

Then he pushed his index finger against the screen of the tablet he was holding, and the luggage cart pulled away with a soft whir. "Your suitcase will be transferred to your compartment automatically," he said. "You will be staying in Suite 6, in the second car from the front. May I ask when to expect your companion, Ms. Küfer?"

Her companion. Penny bit her lower lip.

"I'm traveling alone," she said, trying hard to make those words sound casual. She'd succeeded quite well, she thought. Anyway, the steward nodded as a matter of course, wished her a pleasant trip, and then she was already on her way to her compartment.

I'm traveling alone. She would have to get used to those words for the foreseeable future. It had been three days since Stefan, her fiancé, had left her. And before that... oh, well...

Only twelve hours prior to her dreams of love being shattered, her mother had officially disinherited her. What a great week!

Of course, strictly speaking Penny herself was to blame for both calamities, but still she felt betrayed. What had she done that had been so terrible? Nothing more than to finally follow the dream that she had been carrying around in her heart since she was a little girl.

Exactly one week ago she had started training at the Argus Academy: she had enrolled in the fifteen-week course to become a professional detective.

In her mother's eyes, that was apparently akin to being infected with leprosy. Frederike Küfer was only interested in one thing—prestige. No, wait, that wasn't quite correct.

First, her name was no longer Küfer, but *Princess von Waldenstein*. Frederike had recently married for the fourth time, and her new husband was the offspring of an old noble family. And second, money was at least as important as prestige in Frederike's eyes, no doubt about it. But she had already amassed so much of it during her first marriage that it wasn't really an issue anymore.

Frederike had been planning the same type of life for her daughter and had never made a secret of this fact. Getting married to a member of high society—such as the heartless Stefan—and producing one or two pretty children, getting on the board of a few charities... anything but a career as a professional sleuth! What a disgrace!

Penny still felt sick when she thought about the last conversation she'd had with her mother. But she would manage alright on her own, without the financial support that Frederike had so generously showered upon her up until now. Penny had not been living in blatant luxury, but very comfortably, without ever having to worry about how she was going to pay her next month's rent.

But still, she would not surrender. Never, ever! Giving in and crawling back to Mommy full of remorse was out of the question. No, she would complete her training and acquire all the knowledge a good investigator needed. Then she would gain a few years of experience as the employee of an established detective agency, and finally realize her dream of becoming a professional private eye.

She was certainly aware that in the real world of the 21st century the job did not necessarily compare to the lives and adventures of her greatest idols. Hercule Poirot, Sherlock Holmes, Inspector Maigret, Miss Marple, Inspector Columbo—Penny would probably never be able to work the kind of cases these master sleuths had routinely solved. More probably she would have to spy on unfaithful husbands, hunt down thieving employees, and maybe search for a missing poodle occasionally.

Nonetheless, she was living her dream, and even the first week of training had been an exciting adventure. She had taken her first tentative steps in criminology, had started to study the relevant laws and had learned the basics of the psychology of criminals. She had soaked up all this knowledge like a dry bath sponge.

This weekend's trip that she had been looking forward to for a very long time, the journey on the Occident Express, would probably be her last luxury outing for years to come. Fortunately she had already paid for it when she booked the trip. From now on she would have to tightly manage her budget. No longer would she be able to whip out the platinum credit card her mother had given her.

I'm going to enjoy this trip to the fullest, she decided—even without the company of her faithless fiancé. She loved trains almost as much as she did detective stories, and the Occident Express was the crown jewel as far as luxury trains were concerned. Not only in Europe, but in the whole world.

They would be on the road—no, on the rails—for a whole fourteen hours, overnight, from Vienna to Paris. The train was designed for a maximum speed of 280 kilometers per hour; Penny had read that on the website of the Occident Express. But it usually travelled at a much slower pace, because the trip was not about arriving as quickly as possible at the destination, but about enjoying every minute of the ride. The journey was its own reward, as the saying went.

Like a glittering snake of frozen mercury, the train with its bullet-shaped engine and six cars stretched along the platform. It was perfectly streamlined, and its outer shell was made of some high-tech metal and lots of glass. The cars had huge panoramic windows, which could be transformed from transparent to milky as needed, and the roof of the train was similarly glass-covered and equally transformable. All it took was the push of a button. Penny had learned that, too, from the train company's website. Surely there would be a magnificent view of the starry sky when the lights in the cabin were dimmed at night.

She had just reached the car the steward had pointed out to her, and was preparing to enter it, when the man uttered what could only be described as a cry of joy.

Penny stumbled and wheeled around.

2

"Mrs. Salmann, welcome!" the steward exclaimed. "How nice to finally meet you in person. And your family, too!" The steward beamed with enthusiasm and excitedly shook the hands of the people who had gathered in front of him.

Penny counted seven: three men, four women—and then she suddenly knew why the name *Salmann* sounded familiar. She had met the tall gray-haired lady at the head of the group before, on more than one occasion—at her mother's dinner parties, frequented by high society, at art openings and at exclusive charity events. She was clearly in charge of the others.

This woman ranked in a top spot within the elite. Her name was Madeleine Salmann, the owner of the Occident Express. She lived in Paris and was one of the most famous businesswomen in Europe, even though she had long since passed seventy. She was a technical genius, almost a living legend. In the media, she had already been compared to Elon Musk, Thomas Edison or even Nikola Tesla. She was invested in various industries, from tunnel and power plant construction, to vehicles and armaments, to space travel.

Madame Salmann had launched the Occident Express a few years previously, sparing neither expense nor effort. The ultra-modern luxury train was to be the modern counterpart to the legendary Orient Express, but it traveled west instead of to the Orient, and critics agreed that it far surpassed its famous predecessor in terms of extravagance and comfort. It was common knowledge that Madeleine Salmann also used her beloved train for her own travels whenever possible.

Penny wondered if she should greet the woman. Surely the famous inventor would remember her. Penny's striking red hair and the fact that her impulsive manner often made her look like a bull in a china shop within the bounds of high society also had their advantages. She was vividly remembered by most people she met. And just because she had fallen out of favor with her mother didn't mean she had to break with all of her mom's friends and acquaintances.

Members of high society were just the sort of people who might someday be in need of a good detective. It was never too early to secure future clients.

So Penny waited until Madeleine came her way on the platform. The people accompanying the entrepreneur walked in front of the old lady. The steward had greeted them as *family,* but each of them seemed intent on putting as much distance between themselves and the others as possible. Especially when it came to Madeleine. The old lady formed the tail end of the group, except for a woman in a very conservative business suit who walked behind her at a respectful distance.

No, wait. There was one more woman, right at Madeleine's side: a very young and attractive black-haired woman, who had arrived arm in arm with one of the men. Now, however, she had linked arms with the old lady and walked beside her. She was chatting, smiling and seemingly in the best of moods.

Penny noted with satisfaction that already, after her first week of training, she was able to see the world with different eyes. With the eyes of a detective! She perceived what was happening around her, memorized new surroundings and the faces of the people she met, and observed as attentively as possible when something unusual occurred in her presence.

The way these people in the company of Madeleine Salmann avoided each other fell into the latter category. Their behavior was unusual. No—disconcerting, rather.

It seemed they hated each another, or at least wanted nothing to do with their family members. The young woman on Madeleine's arm, on the other hand, seemed all too concerned about the old lady. Her friendliness and good humor did not seem authentic.

But one should not jump to conclusions too hastily either. Penny already knew that much.

She put on a smile and approached the old woman when only a few feet separated them on the platform.

"Madame Salmann, do you remember me?" Penny asked her in German, her mother tongue. She knew the entrepreneur spoke fluent German also, even though Madame Salmann was originally French.

Madeleine's husband, who had died much too young, had been Austrian. The Occident Express ran the Vienna-Paris route in his honor, the old lady herself had once told Penny at a cocktail party. Madeleine's voice had been full of melancholy when she had spoken of her husband. The two had met on a train ride when they were both still students, and Penny had secretly wished to also find such a partner one day. A man she could love so much for such a long time, ideally, without losing him prematurely.

Madame Salmann stopped in front of Penny, eyed her suspiciously for a moment, but then her features brightened. "Penelope, isn't it? Well, this is a surprise. Are you a guest on the Express tonight?"

Penny nodded.

The austerely dressed woman in a business suit who had followed Madeleine came to a halt at the same moment as the old lady and remained motionless in the background. The young woman, on the other hand, who had clung to Madeleine's arm in such an overly good mood, would probably have preferred to keep walking. She shifted from one foot to the other and nodded a wordless greeting to Penny.

"How nice," said Madame Salmann. "A wonderful coincidence. Which suite are you in, Penelope?"

"Number 6."

"Very well, then I won't be surrounded exclusively by losers and harpies tonight after all." The old woman made a derogatory hand gesture in the direction of her companions, who had just boarded the train a few meters ahead. At the same time, her voice was so loud that her words were impossible to miss. "You must join me for dinner, my dear Penelope."

"I'd love to. But please, call me Penny." She glanced after the two men who were just climbing the steps of the front car. Both had winced briefly at Madeleine's derogatory words, but hadn't turned or answered the insult in any way. Apparently they didn't want to mess with the old lady. Or were they used to this kind of treatment?

At second glance, the two looked like Madeleine. And they were the right age to be the sons of the old matriarch; somewhere between their late forties and early fifties. Penny was sure, however, that she had never met them at any social occasion.

She felt compassion for the two men. Her own mother had often treated her as if she were a servant. No, a slave. But at least that was over now. From now on, Frederike could bully husband number four, but not her daughter anymore.

The old lady raised an eyebrow. "*Penny*? Fine... if you prefer that." A thin smile played around her lips, almost as if she sympathized with that nickname.

Madeleine was not exactly a very progressive name

either, but still a thousand times better than *Penelope*. And Madame Salmann was the right age for it. In her youth, *Madeleine* might have sounded cool and modern.

"I'll see you later, then," the old lady added. She started moving again, passing Penny and heading for the first train car. The beautiful black-haired woman stayed by her side and started chatting again. She talked about train journeys she had already taken and emphasized several times how much she liked the Occident Express.

The woman in the business suit, on the other hand, who had remained in the background until now, stepped in front of Penny and extended her hand. "I'm Christiane Schneiders, Madame Salmann's assistant," she said.

But then her boss stopped a few meters ahead, turned to Schneiders and raised her eyebrows imperiously. Which probably meant something like: *Don't dawdle. Follow me.*

A pained smile flitted across the assistant's face. She might have been around forty, wore her white-blond hair in a perfectly-parted pageboy cut and was apparently very eager to serve. Without another word, she hurried after her mistress.

Penny turned and climbed into her own train car. This could develop into an interesting evening; surely there would be plenty of opportunities for her to practice her observation and deduction skills. Not quite the romantic trip with her fiancé she had dreamed of, but still better than hanging out alone in her luxury suite, wallowing in self-pity, and moping the whole way.

3

On the Occident Express, shortly after Vienna
7:10 pm

"You've got to man up, Martin," Erika Salmann said, giving her husband a disparaging look. She sat very upright on the queen size bed of their compartment. Her feet rested on a midnight-blue damask blanket decorated with the Occident Express's logo: a bullet-shaped silver locomotive with two mighty wings growing out of its fuselage.

Erika hated the logo, just as she hated the confounded train she had to board every year on the anniversary of her father-in-law's death—just because Madeleine, the old dragon, insisted on it. Erika definitely detested Martin's mother more than anyone else in the world.

She eyed her husband, who was sitting motionless at the small desk in their compartment with his shoulders slumped. He was staring through the huge panoramic window at the passing lights of the city. The Occident Express had started its journey only a few minutes before.

Martin always reacted like that when she reproached him. He ducked his head and kept quiet. And what infuriated her the most was that she knew that her sermons were completely in vain. Martin would never stand up to his mother. More likely that hell would freeze over. The old woman was twice as intelligent as he was and wouldn't let anything or anyone get her down, especially not her eldest son, in whom she saw the biggest failure in the family. Unfortunately, Erika had to agree with her.

"What should I do in your opinion, darling?" asked Martin cautiously. "Do you want me to just march into Mom's office and demand a vice president's salary? That wouldn't be fair towards the other team managers, would it?"

"What's not fair is that you, her son, have such a tiny job in the company. You should be on the board, damn it! And earn a proper salary. I'm tired of living like a beggar."

"Come on now! We live on one of the most beautiful estates in all of France!"

Erika couldn't believe that he'd dared to contradict her. Maybe there was still hope, and he would finally gain some confidence. Maybe he just needed to be pushed a bit more?

Well, that wasn't a problem. "We live in your mother's house," Erika said, putting on a particularly venomous look. "And she's keeping you on an allowance like you're a ten-year-old boy!"

"I'll make it to department head in a few years," Martin said. "You know I'm trying hard. But you believe it's all so easy. I'm not a genius like Mother. For her, things can't be challenging enough. While I'm not exactly a tech wiz—"

"Yes, yes, all right," Erika interrupted him. "You're having a hard time with technology. I've heard that a hundred times."

"Because it's true. I never claimed to be a prodigy. I thought you'd married me because—"

He fell silent and stared out the window again. Just like he didn't understand any more what exactly Erika had once seen in him. For the life of her, she couldn't remember it herself.

"You'll just have to market yourself better, Martin," she urged him, now striving for a more conciliatory tone. "Just look at your brothers. Two good-for-nothings, if I ever met any. You, at least, have achieved a position in your mother's company. You've got to finally get her to sign a succession agreement—in your favor."

"I'll talk to her," he promised, sounding so hopeless that Erika groaned in exasperation. What a loser! She couldn't rely on him. It was high time to take matters into her own hands.

Jacques Salmann had made himself comfortable on the bed in his compartment. He was reading a daily newspaper when the door opened.

Louise, his beautiful black-haired fiancée, came in. She was smiling and in a good mood. She looked as if they were about to embark on the trip of a lifetime. For some unknown reason she seemed to have taken a liking to this bourgeois palace on wheels, and to his mother, who had already fawned over Louise on their way to Vienna as if she were *her* bride-to-be and not his. Why was Louise so friendly with the old witch? What was she up to?

Louise snapped him out of his thoughts. She performed a pirouette at the foot of the bed and exclaimed, "Isn't it wonderful, darling? I love this train! We should travel on the Occident Express much more often!"

"Certainly not," Jacques growled. It was enough for him to meet with his mother the few times a year that family events made unavoidable, occasions he used wisely to raise new funds for his travels. At least she wasn't stingy, his otherwise heartless mother—if you knew how to wheedle her, you could squeeze enough money out of her.

Well, he never asked for more than she could pay out of petty cash. After all, she was one of the richest women in France.

Jacques just didn't need much. He was the frugal type. The decadence of this train or his family's palace disgusted him. As did Martin, his older brother, and his eternally nagging wife, who were sucking up to Mother just so they could live a life of glamour and comfort—and convince themselves that they belonged in high society.

Jacques had actually assumed that Louise saw these matters the same way he did. After all, she had already proven to him several times that she was fond of travel and adventure far from civilization, just like he was. So why the hell was she sucking up to the old witch now? What was she up to?

He had already asked her about it on the way to Vienna, but all he had gotten out of her was that she admired his mother. "I've never met such an intelligent woman," Louise had raved, "I can't believe all she's accomplished. All those trains, planes, machines and robots she's developed—"

"Not to mention the tanks. Or the drones," Jacques had interrupted her. But it hadn't helped. Apparently, Louise had no moral qualms whatsoever about the arms trade.

Today, she had been fawning over the old witch yet again. Just now, on the platform, she had left him standing there like a stranger, and hooked up with Madeleine as if she were her best friend.

I'll end up being jealous of my own mother, Jacques told himself bitterly. But he would not let it come to that.

Xavier Salmann, the youngest of the three brothers, stood in the corridor outside his compartment and looked over at the door with the number 6.

The girl who had just disappeared in there.... she

was exactly according to his taste. Red-haired and pale-skinned like an elf, with bright blue eyes that looked so innocent. He was sure, however, that Penny—he had picked up her name earlier on the platform—was anything but innocent. And if she were, he'd spoil her tonight, his beautiful neighbor on the train.

Apparently, she knew his mother, even seemed to like her, the ossified old woman who possessed about as much charm as the robots that rolled off the assembly line in her factories. At least, the effusive greeting Penny had just given the old hag on the platform had made that impression on him.

But Xavier didn't care. Let Penny dine at ease with Mother; the young redhead would find her way to his compartment by bedtime at the latest. He would see to that. He was not only far more attractive than his older brothers, but he also knew how to treat women. How to make himself desirable, no, irresistible, as a man and get everything he wanted from any female he chose. Sex, money, valuable connections, whatever they had to offer.

Xavier wasn't picky, and his loot was plentiful enough that he didn't need to constantly beg his mother for money the way Martin and Jacques did.

How he despised them, the two weaklings. No idea who they had taken after—their father had not been such a wimp. Xavier, on the other hand, was cut from very different cloth. He was smart like his mother, and he could be just as ruthless when it was called for. But he didn't waste his gifts on a seventy-hour workweek at a stupid company. He possessed savoir-vivre; he knew how to enjoy the finer things in life. And he would not let anything or anyone take that away from him!

The fact that Penny was an acquaintance of his mother and could afford a ride on the Occident Express could only mean one thing: she was certainly from a very wealthy home. All the more reason to make her acquaintance. Good sex and a bulging bank account were an exceedingly exciting mixture.

4

Penny looked out the window of her compartment, but could see nothing except the walls of a passing tunnel. Although the concrete cladding of the narrow tube reflected sound and thus amplified it many times over, there was hardly any driving noise from the ultra-modern train. The Occident Express seemed to be literally floating through the night.

The interior of Penny's compartment, however, was more reminiscent of a luxury hotel from long ago than a hypermodern train, and it was exceedingly spacious. Only three suites were housed in one car, so you didn't sleep on narrow beds that were converted into bench seats during the day, as was common on other trains. Instead there was a queen size bed with an extra high mattress, with the finest down comforters and a sheet so smooth it felt like silk.

The other side of the room was occupied by a comfortable designer sofa for two, and under the panoramic window there was a fine wooden desk with brass-covered legs. In addition, the suite had its own fully-equipped bathroom. Penny had never seen anything like it on a train. Madeleine Salmann had really made a luxury dream come true on rails with her Occident Express.

On the wall next to the cabin door was a futuristic control panel that caught Penny's attention. *Onboard Service* read the headline on the touch screen, and below it were buttons for various amenities. *Drinks, Snacks, Housekeeping, Emergencies...*

Penny was actually perfectly happy in her compartment, but wanted to give the panel a try. So she selected *Housekeeping*, scrolled through various options for making her stay on board even more pleasant, and finally decided on an extra bolster. One slept well on it—and she really had no use for extra towels, bath slippers or another cashmere blanket. After all, the compartment was very generously equipped for two people, not a solo traveler.

She tapped the icon for the bolster, and didn't have to wait long for it. Less than two minutes after she had placed her order, a dignified *Doooong* sounded—which was probably meant to represent a doorbell.

Penny opened her door, expecting to face a steward who would hand her the bolster. Her expectation was disappointed, however, and she looked out into the deserted corridor, lit with warm yellow light.

But then something beeped, right at her feet. Penny's gaze wandered downward—and she let out a surprised gasp. At about knee height, a robot stood opposite her. It was silver-gray, roundish, and no bigger than a poodle. In addition, it was equipped with wheels and had two camera eyes at the front, giving it a remotely humanoid appearance. Stowed in its gripper arms was the bolster that Penny had ordered.

The robot focused its camera eyes on her and reported in an electronic voice, "Your order, Ms. Küfer. Here you are." Then he lifted his arms and Penny accepted the bolster with her mouth open.

"Is there anything else I can do for you, Ms. Küfer?"

"Uh, no... thank you."

"Then I wish you a pleasant journey."

Wow, Penny thought.

The electronic valet was already rolling back down the hallway when she heard a dark female voice behind her. "Do you like it?"

She turned around and looked into the amused face of Madeleine Salmann. The cute little robot, which looked as cuddly as a pet, was certainly a product of her company. Maybe even one of her own creations.

"He's great," Penny said. "I'd love to order the whole service menu up and down right now just to have him come back again!"

The old lady smiled. "Don't hold back, Penelope. That's what it's there for." She winked and her lips formed into a smile.

Behind Madame Salmann, Penny saw the assistant, Christiane Schneiders, who was still dressed in her formal gray business suit, while her boss was now wearing a floor-length, midnight blue silk dress. Almost as if she had an appointment for an evening at the opera.

At that moment, the door of compartment number 5, the one right next to Penny's, opened. Out stepped a hellishly handsome man, whom she had noticed on the platform earlier before the train left. He belonged to Madame Salmann's family, she guessed, even if he had kept aloof. At least he had arrived together with the old lady and the other members of her small group.

Madeleine gave him a quick look that could only be described as icy, then turned back to Penny. "Come, my dear, accompany me to the restaurant. I don't want to end up spending the evening with one of my wayward sons."

The man, who stood a good five foot nine and might have been in his early forties, ignored his mother's spite, moved a few steps down the aisle, and greeted Penny like a long-lost friend. "How nice to meet a friendly face on this Polar Express," he said in a pleasantly warm voice, at the same time grasping Penny's hand. "I am Xavier Salmann—most pleased to make your acquaintance, Mademoiselle."

He playfully indicated a bow. His German was almost without accent. "Perhaps we can get to know each other better later," he continued, "when my dear Mother has finished with you. I'm sure you'll feel the need for *human* companionship, then."

He gave Penny a beaming smile, then nimbly squeezed between the two women and walked down the aisle toward the lounge car, which lay between the front passenger cars and the restaurant.

The old lady screwed up her face, then turned to her assistant. "Schneiders, go ahead and see that we have a table to ourselves. As far away from my brood as possible," she added.

The assistant did as she was told and hurried after Xavier Salmann, while Madeleine linked arms with Penny. The aisle was barely wide enough for the two women to walk side by side, but slender as they both were they managed it in the end. Madeleine strode through her train like a queen, and Penny wondered what kind of family drama she had gotten herself into. Why did people, who seemed to hate each other as much as the Salmanns did, go traveling together?

5

Shortly after St. Pölten
7:45 pm

"Quite simple, my dear," Madeleine answered her question after they had settled down at a table at the front end of the restaurant car. Of course, Penny had phrased her inquiry more diplomatically than the thought that had popped into her head: "What brought you and your family to Vienna, Mrs. Salmann? All together, when you're, um, not that close to each other?"

"The twenty-second anniversary of my husband's death," Madeleine answered wistfully. "He insisted on being buried in Vienna—in his hometown. I complied with that wish, of course, and we have visited his grave every year since. My sons and I; their love for their father was much greater than for me, you must know. It's no secret, but I don't care. They are good-for-nothings, all of them, and apart from this one trip each and every year, I only get to see them when they need money. Well, except for Martin, who works in my company. I'm permanently stuck with him, but at least I was able to place him in a position where he can't do any harm. Isn't that right, Schneiders?" She glanced at the secretary sitting to her left.

The latter nodded wordlessly while her gaze rested on the smartphone lying on the table next to her. It vibrated gently.

"Excuse me," Schneiders said, standing up and moving away from the table. She didn't get far, because the train car came to an end just a meter and a half away.

Schneiders squeezed herself into the corner as best she could, turned her back, and spoke into the phone in a hushed voice. As far as Penny could make out her words, she was talking about a production delay at one of Madame Salmann's factories.

Madeleine stared at her assistant's back. "A loyal soul, the good Schneiders," she commented. "She's been keeping the small stuff off my neck for many years, is quite capable, and doesn't shy away from unusual working hours. A gifted autodidact as far as my line of work is concerned. She doesn't even have a graduate degree, but she is quite smart. Occasionally though, I do have to remind her where her place is."

Unusual working hours? Penny thought silently. Apparently, that meant around the clock. From the looks of it, the assistant even accompanied her demanding boss on trips and still had to deal with phone calls while Madeleine was already devoting herself to dinner.

"What had we just been talking about?" said the old lady. "Oh, yes, my dear sons."

She shrugged, her evening robe rustling. "They are

my flesh and blood, after all. All I have left of my husband."

"You can't choose your family," Penny replied with more bitterness than she had intended—and before she knew it she was pouring her heart out to Madame Salmann about her own family crisis.

Even before the main course was served, she had confessed everything to Madeleine—that her mother had disinherited her, that her fiancé had abandoned her—but also that she was determined to pursue a career as a detective nevertheless. It felt good to get things off her chest, and the old lady turned out to be an amazingly patient listener.

Christiane Schneiders only ever spent a few minutes at the table, then her smartphone vibrated again and she retreated back to her corner. The competence she exuded was quite impressive. After half an hour, Penny didn't even notice any more if the assistant was sitting at the table or quietly whispering away in her corner. Penny talked, and ate, and drank delicious wine, and the more the evening progressed, the more she was able to relax.

It had been a good idea to take this train ride alone, she told herself. She didn't need a man, especially not one who would abandon her so shamefully just because she was pursuing an unusual career path. Or because she had been disinherited by her mother? Why exactly her fiancé suddenly hadn't wanted her anymore, he hadn't told her. And she sure as hell wasn't going to ask him about it! She would never exchange a word with that snob again. Let him marry some dolled-up socialite and be bored to death with her until the end of his days!

All the tables in the dining room were occupied. The train seemed to be fully booked, which didn't surprise Penny. The fare was astronomically high, but there was no shortage of people in the world who didn't know how to spend all their money. Madame Salmann's family members sat spread out across the room, among the passengers from the two rear coaches. Even at dinner they seemed intent on keeping the maximum possible distance from each other—and from their mother.

Madeleine turned to her assistant, who had just returned from another phone call. As far as Penny had noticed, the poor woman had not yet had a chance to eat anything, while her employer was already enjoying the second main course.

"Schneiders, why don't you check and see if we have any positions to fill on our security team," Madeleine said. "My young friend here is a budding detective and seems to me to be extremely dedicated. Just the kind of employee we always like to hire, isn't she?"

The assistant looked at Penny, impressed. "A detective?" she repeated.

Penny nodded. She had no intention of becoming an employee in any company, even though Madame Salmann's corporate group was certainly active in exciting fields of activity—but she also didn't want to be rude and flatly refuse the old lady's friendly offer.

Schneiders typed something into her cell phone—presumably making a note about the job for Penny—then finally managed to eat the appetizer and join the conversation at the table for a bit. She was a good listener, too, and behind her stern exterior she was actually very friendly and gracious. And quite pretty at second glance, Penny thought. Probably the kind of career woman who didn't waste any thought on makeup, jewelry, or other feminine accessories because of her zeal for work.

Suddenly, however, Schneiders raised both eyebrows and stared over Penny's shoulder. Her look seemed so suspicious that Penny inevitably had to turn around.

At the table in the assistant's field of vision sat Martin Salmann and his wife, whose first name Penny had not yet picked up. The somewhat stocky-looking woman, who had donned a multi-strand pearl necklace, might be the same age as her husband, in her early fifties perhaps. She seemed to have just put something into her handbag, which she now hung back on the armrest of her chair. Then she turned her attention back to her food.

Had Martin's wife been the one to arouse Christiane Schneiders' suspicions? Penny turned again to the assistant, but Schneiders was just rising again from the table. Another call was coming in on her work phone, which she answered without hesitation.

Maybe I was just imagining things, Penny told herself. There had been nothing unusual about this small incident. A woman reaching for her own purse—what could be more commonplace? But still, the secretary had looked almost disturbed.

Had Schneiders not been watching Martin Salmann and his wife, but someone else, further back in the room? There were passengers from the rear carriages, travelers who didn't belong to Madame Salmann's family. What could the assistant have seen that had astonished her so much?

You're getting a little carried away with honing your observation skills, Penny admonished herself. *Give it a rest. There aren't secrets or even crimes lurking everywhere just because you're a detective now.*

Okay, she was just a *budding* detective who was still at the very beginning of her training. But nevertheless she decided to relax some more and enjoy the evening. She reached for her wine glass, smiled at Madame Salmann and took a big sip.

6

Between Linz and Salzburg
9:20 pm

Barely fifteen minutes after dessert had been served, Madeleine Salmann announced that she was feeling very sleepy and wanted to retire.

"But please, my dear, don't mind me. I want you to have a wonderful evening," she told Penny. "Try some of our cocktails, here in the restaurant or next door in the lounge car. You'll be delighted. And you are, of course, my guest tonight!"

Penny wanted to protest, but the old lady waved it off and was on her feet the next moment. Schneiders also jumped up from her chair and left the restaurant together with her boss.

Penny remained behind alone. *A cocktail, then,* she told herself. She looked around the restaurant. There were almost only couples sitting at the round tables. Most had already finished dinner and were now putting their heads together over a cup of coffee or a glass of dessert wine.

The murmur of their conversations enveloped Penny, their laughter reached her ears, and the air was filled with the tempting smell of the various desserts which were just being served in her immediate neighborhood. Warm chocolate cake, tiramisu, apple strudel with vanilla sauce—Penny would have loved to order another of the sweet delicacies right away, even though she had already devoured a large piece of walnut cake.

She managed to resist the temptation and decided to go next door, to the lounge car that she had already passed through before on her way to the restaurant. The sight of all those couples was getting to her. It was clearly too much romance and harmony for tonight.

She stood up and crossed the airlock between the two carriages. Like all passages in the train, it was permanently open and lined with some shiny, metallic, high-tech material. One almost had the feeling of being in a spaceship.

On entering the lounge car, however, she found it exuded the same old-fashioned charm as the restaurant car and the passenger suites. It was laid out with a discreetly patterned carpet, furnished with inviting leather fauteuils and elegant little wooden tables, and was so artfully lit that one felt like a guest in some fairytale palace.

Oil paintings hung on the walls between the huge panoramic panes, all showing a similar motif—albeit from completely different historical eras. They were pictures of locomotives or entire trains winding their way across bold bridges, puffing over steep mountain passes under great clouds of steam, or crossing dark, seemingly endless forests. A hymn to rail travel.

Penny was the only guest in the lounge, but that would surely change over the course of the evening. A waiter in immaculate black livery hurried over, followed by one of the cute robots that also did duty in the passenger compartments.

"This is Fred, your personal butler," the flesh-and-blood waiter introduced his electronic colleague. "If you want nuts, chocolates, a newspaper... just call him by name and he'll be with you right away. You can just let him know your order. No pushing of any buttons is required. I, on the other hand, will take care of your beverage requests. Do you already know what you'd like, or can I bring you the bar menu?"

Penny gazed at Fred, who seemed to be watching her from his camera-lens eyes, then ordered a cappuccino from the waiter.

The man hurried away, while the robot retreated discreetly towards the wall beneath one of the paintings. Penny counted two more of the little gadgets waiting for guests further back in the lounge car. It was fascinating and at the same time a little creepy to be waited upon by these artificial intelligences.

When Penny lifted her eyes and looked through the glass roof of the train, right into the night sky, she noticed that it had begun to snow. Thick flakes were falling from the clouds and dancing around the train in a wild rhythm. Penny felt wonderfully warm and secure in the elegant parlor car and sank deeper into the comfortable upholstery of her fauteuil.

The waiter served her the coffee, she added two sweetener tablets and then closed her eyes and listened to the barely perceptible sound of the train. The Occident Express glided along at a leisurely pace, at best half the speed it was technically capable of, Penny estimated. She was enjoying this almost nostalgic form of travel, which was not about the otherwise so-important *faster, further, higher of* modern times.

"Mind if I join you?" a man's voice cut quite abruptly into her dreamy contemplations. Penny flinched and opened her eyes.

"Oh, I beg your pardon," the man said, but at the same time he took a seat, unbidden, in the armchair to Penny's left. Then he fixed his warm brown eyes on her.

He looked at her in the same way one generally looked at a particularly interesting work of art. Very focused and with obvious pleasure.

It was Xavier Salmann, Madeleine's youngest son, who with his good looks could easily have passed for a movie star. His dark hair was grayish at the temples, his chin angular and masculine, his hands strong but well-groomed.

Penny felt her pulse quicken. Reflexively, she wanted to brush him off, but then she remembered that she was a single woman now. Unattached, free, beholden to no one in the whole world. Some attractive company over coffee really couldn't hurt!

So she allowed herself to return Xavier's smile. He made himself comfortable in his armchair, crossed his long legs, and then suddenly called out to Fred.

It took Penny a moment to remember who that was: the cuddly little service robot. Within seconds he'd purred up, and Xavier ordered roasted almonds from him as if it were the most natural thing in the world. The waiter, who arrived at the table shortly after Fred, brought him a double whiskey, and then Xavier turned his full attention to Penny.

She let him engage her in small talk, which soon turned into quite salacious banter. Following her coffee, she ordered a cocktail, gazed into the stunning eyes of her companion, listened to his flattery, which was amazingly creative, and watched the snowflakes dancing outside the windows.

Just as the train made a brief stop under the glass domed roof of Salzburg's main station, the attractive black-haired woman who had caught Penny's eye on the platform in Vienna entered the lounge car. It was the same young woman who had hooked up with Madeleine Salmann and tried so hard to radiate good humor. Now she was holding the hand of a man who looked remotely like Xavier, even if he was far less attractive. Penny had already seen him, too, at the train station in Vienna. Now it was clear to her that this man had to be one of Xavier's older brothers.

"My dearest brother," Xavier called out, as if to confirm her realization, and beckoned the two newcomers closer. The enthusiasm in his voice was so clearly insincere that it seemed almost grotesque. "Had enough of dining already, you two? Retiring to your compartment for some horizontal pleasure among fiancés? That's an excellent idea."

Turning to Penny, he added, "May I introduce Jacques, my beloved brother. He's the middle one of the three of us. And Louise, his lovely fiancée. By God, I can't explain to you what she sees in him, but she is determined to marry him. Or have you come to your senses by now, beautiful girl?"

He scrutinized Louise intently, as if he really could not believe that she actually wanted to marry Jacques. She, however, abruptly turned her head away and looked at the floor.

A strange reaction, Penny thought. Of course, Louise couldn't be blamed for finding Xavier's remarks more embarrassing than funny, but there seemed to be more to this seemingly shy lowering of her gaze.

Are you again seeing connections where none exist? Penny admonished herself. She wasn't sure, but before she could study Louise's expression more closely, Jacques was already pulling her away with him. Without so much as one word to Xavier, he strode away and steered his fiancée between the now mostly occupied tables of the lounge car. They disappeared at the other end through the airlock that led to the front sleeping cars of the train.

"Jacques has zero sense of humor," Xavier comment-ed, glancing after his brother. "Or any taste for the finer things in life. He's happiest when he's fighting his way through some snake's nest in the middle of nowhere or risking his neck in the latest trendy sport."

He shook his head disapprovingly, but then some-thing gentle, almost wistful, flitted across his hand-some features. "He's the only one of the three of us who looks like my father," he said to Penny, who was eyeing him intensely. "He's the spitting image of our old man." Xavier sighed. "I miss him sometimes, you know. He was the best father you could ever ask for. Unfortunately, we lost him way too soon."

"Was he sick, then?" asked Penny gently. It surprised her to see this empathetic side Xavier was suddenly displaying. After only a few minutes of their acquaint-ance, it had become clear to her that Madeleine's youngest offspring was a reckless philanderer and womanizer.

Not that she was particularly bothered by that. For a carefree evening, such a man was exactly the right one. He knew how to woo a woman, and there was no danger of falling in love with such a guy. Penny had had enough of love for now. *For a long time,* she told herself silently.

Xavier shook his head and looked at her with a pained expression in his beautiful eyes. "He was gunned down. In the open street, just a few hundred meters from our house."

Penny, astonished, set down the cocktail glass she had just sipped from. "A murder? That's awful. Did they catch whoever did it?"

"No," Xavier replied. "They assumed it was a robbery. Dad's watch and wallet were missing when he was found. The killer, however, was never identified. But forgive me, my pretty, that's really not a topic of conversation for such a wonderful evening."

He reached for his glass, swirling its contents back and forth and making the ice cubes clink gently. Then he put the Prince Charming mask that Penny had already come to know well that evening back on. "What do you say," he asked, "let's go somewhere cozy where it's just the two of us?"

7

Shortly before Innsbruck
11:40 pm

With skillful hands, Xavier uncorked the champagne bottle that one of the cute service robots had just delivered to Penny's compartment. He was generally not interested in his mother's work, didn't fancy her crazy inventions, all the technical stuff—but with these little guys she had really succeeded for once, in his eyes.

With an ice bucket and champagne bottle in his left steel claw, and two slender glass goblets in his right, the little robot had arrived—and didn't even expect a tip.

Xavier filled both glasses to the brim with champagne, then turned to his conquest, who had already made herself comfortable on the bed. He looked at her closely as he approached her almost in slow motion. And he was very pleased with what he saw.

This Penelope Küfer was quite a hot kitten: lively, spirited, with a feminine but not too voluptuous figure. Just the way he liked it. All right, she talked a bit much, and with the speed of a machine gun at that, but he could handle it. Women loved a good listener, so he was willing to put up with her chatter.

Patiently, he had listened to half the life story of his

new conquest, earlier in the lounge car. He had learned that Penny dreamed of becoming a great detective, which was rather naïve for his taste. She had also confided in him that her fiancé had dumped her just because he didn't think that kind of profession was befitting his future bride. What a snoot! But Xavier was only too happy to step in as a comforter. And finally, Penny had complained that her mother—a multimillionaire—had disinherited her, which was a shame, since it precluded a longer acquaintance with the hot little redhead.

Xavier did not waste himself on mediocre conquests. Only women who could invite him on stylish trips, pamper him in the best restaurants, and give him expensive watches as gifts were able to enjoy his acquaintance for any length of time. After all, he was not exclusively concerned with pleasure; he also had to make a living.

So Penny was only a girl for tonight's bedtime, but she would do very well in that role. Xavier had no doubt about it. Even if she was still fully dressed—but he would soon change that.

It was her compartment they were staying in. He had suggested accompanying her here for tactical reasons, because that way he could withdraw when he had had enough of her. Which could take a few hours.

He was about to hand Penny one of the champagne goblets and join her on the bed, when it happened—something tickled his Achilles tendon, as if an ant were crawling there, and the next moment a burning pain shot through his foot.

The champagne goblets almost slipped from his hands, so awful was this sensation. He stumbled. What the hell...?

"Xavier?" cried Penny. She nimbly jumped off the bed and grabbed him under the arm. "What's wrong?"

"I don't know, something bit me. Or stung? It hurts like hell, anyway. Are there bugs on Maman's luxury train, or what?" He cursed, then pressed both glasses into Penny's hands and bent down.

He rolled up his right pants leg, pushed the sock down as far as he could, and tried to figure out what had hurt him. The pain in his foot spread like liquid fire, relentless and furiously fast.

For her part, Penny got down on her knees and stared at the exposed patch of skin.

"There are two tiny holes," she said, pointing her index finger at his burning wound. Her face reflected a mixture of surprise and concern.

It was almost a little touching. He was used to reading passion and desire in the faces of his women, but not this—not this expression of genuine compassion.

Don't get sentimental now, dude, he admonished himself. But what in the world could cause such nasty pain? He gritted his teeth and looked around the floor of the compartment to see if there was a disgusting insect somewhere. In the softly dimmed light of the bedside lamps, however, nothing was visible.

He straightened up again, hopped toward the bed, putting weight only on his intact leg, and sat down. His entire calf was throbbing now, not just the foot, and the wound was burning as if someone were pouring liquid oil into it.

"What can I do?" Penny asked him. Her voice sounded composed but concerned. "Look at how it's swelling up! I'll call the steward, surely they have a first aid kit or something like that on board. An ointment, perhaps?"

She walked the few steps over to the service panel and tapped the touchscreen, which was in sleep mode. The screen came to life, glowing softly. Xavier could see that she was selecting an icon with her fingertip that depicted a stylized human.

"Personal service," she explained to him. "I don't think any of the robots can help us in this case."

Penny's outline blurred before his eyes. Tears welled up under his eyelids and streamed down his cheeks without him being able to do anything about it.

Jesus Christ! Was he really crying like a sissy now, just because some goddamn vermin had bitten him?

His foot continued to swell, but felt increasingly numb. The pain ate its way up his leg.

He loosened his shirt collar. Damn hot in here. Breathing suddenly became so difficult, as if he had just climbed a mountain peak at a run. Damn it, what was wrong with him?

"Oh God, Xavier!" he heard Penny call out. Her eyes

widened in fear as she stared at him, then suddenly the room spun around and he lost sight of her.

Nausea rose in him; he heard a rasping sound that he only identified as his own breath a few seconds later. It sounded like a decrepit boiler about to explode.

"I guess we'll have to postpone sex," he was still joking—or rather trying to. His jaw muscles no longer obeyed him; his mouth was suddenly full of saliva. He struggled for breath.

Then his field of vision went black.

8

Penny rushed out of her cabin, out into the aisle and screamed for help.

There was no time to wait for any steward who might have a first aid kit available. Xavier had toppled over on the bed, as if gripped by violent nausea. His breaths had degenerated to a gasp, and then it had all been over. Silence. No more breath, no pulse that Penny could find, no matter how thoroughly she palpated Xavier's wrists and finally his neck.

A waiter came rushing from the lounge car, and at the same time the compartment door in the front of her car was pushed open.

Jacques Salmann appeared in the doorway, stared at her questioningly, then came running toward her in long strides.

The waiter reached them almost at the same time. Only a few seconds after him, the steward arrived, probably in response to Penny's call via the service panel.

Damn fast service, it popped into her head, and the next moment she almost laughed hysterically at this ridiculously inappropriate thought.

"I think he's dead," was all she could get out. Her

own voice sounded strangely foreign in her ears. On shaky knees, she followed the three men back into her compartment.

Jacques bent over his brother, who lay motionless, curled up in a fetal position on the bed. The waiter and the steward stood by as if struck by lightning, their eyes staring out of their heads. More footsteps approached in the corridor.

Louise, Jacques Salmann's beautiful fiancée, appeared in the doorway. She stepped into the compartment, and close behind her Martin Salmann pushed in, followed by Schneiders, his mother's dutiful assistant. Thirty seconds later, Martin's wife also appeared and stood on tiptoe to catch a glimpse of the bed.

I have alerted half of the train passengers, Penny thought. But that was a good thing. She hadn't known how to react, all alone with Xavier in her compartment, when he had so suddenly turned from a potential sexual partner into a horribly disfigured corpse.

Jacques Salmann was the first to find his tongue. "What happened here?" he asked, turning to Penny with an accusing expression. He looked around the compartment, staring first at the ice bucket with the champagne bottle in it, then at the two well-filled goblets that now stood on the desk as if forgotten, and finally eyeing Penny with undisguised suspicion in his eyes.

Surely he didn't think she had hurt his brother?

"He was stung. Or bitten," she said quickly, walking over to the bed and pointing at Xavier's foot, which was still half exposed under the rolled-down sock. A deep red swelling had formed around the spot with the two tiny holes.

"Good Lord," said a voice behind her. It belonged to Schneiders, the assistant. "That looks terrible. Is that what he died of?"

"I... think so," Penny said. "It all happened so fast. He suffered a lot of pain, then he got nauseous. And dizzy. And finally—" She left the sentence unfinished. One could see, even without her explanation, what had happened then.

"Was he allergic?" asked Louise, who had pressed herself against her fiancé and was clutching his arm. "You can die from a simple bee sting if you're allergic to it, surely you know that?"

The others nodded in silence.

Penny tried to shake off shock and confusion and get a clear head. "A bee, in December?" she asked. "At night, on a train?"

"Hmm, yeah," Louise muttered. "Not so likely."

Schneiders turned to leave. "I will inform Madame Salmann," she announced in a matter-of-fact tone and was gone the next moment.

Martin addressed the two train crewmen. "You can return to your posts," he announced stiffly. "There's nothing more we can do here. And not a word to the other passengers, will you? We need to handle this

49

professionally. "

He turned to his wife as if to elicit her approval, but she looked straight through him. Her gaze was fixed on the dead man's swollen leg, and she herself had become as pale as if her hours on earth were already numbered as well.

9

Secretly, Penny had to agree with Madeleine's assessment of her sons, even if it was unflattering. Martin, the oldest, clearly felt compelled to take over the crisis command, but was hopelessly overwhelmed by it.

You could literally watch his brain at work behind his high forehead. Excruciatingly slow and not very efficient, Penny thought silently. His mother's IQ must have been twice his. But as yet Schneiders, who had gone to fetch the matriarch, had not returned. Presumably Madeleine was already asleep.

Martin seemed to have no better idea than to wait for his mother. Just like the others, who stood around like pillars of salt in Penny's compartment. She herself had regained her composure, but just couldn't make sense of what had happened to Xavier, even though she had personally witnessed his death at close range.

She pushed through between the bystanders to take another look at the strange wound on Xavier's foot—and suddenly someone cried out. It was Jacques, Martin's younger brother. The next moment he went down on his knees and pulled up his trouser leg.

Penny was overcome with an agonizing sense of déjà vu. She moved toward the middle Salmann scion to get a better look—and bounced back as if against an invisible wall when she caught a glimpse of his foot. There they were again, the two tiny, closely spaced holes. Just like on Xavier's foot before.

Panic broke out among those present. Louise let out a sharp cry, Martin rushed to his brother's aid, grabbed him by the arm and helped him onto the sofa, where he sat down clumsily.

At that moment, Madeleine entered the compartment, closely followed by Schneiders. "What's going on here?" she called out in the tone of a field marshal, but the next moment even she was speechless.

Jacques sat there moaning, his eyes swimming in tears, and he clutched his leg as if to tear it out.

"We need a doctor," Penny called out. "A hospital. You have to stop the train, Mrs. Salmann!"

Madeleine nodded mechanically. "Where are we right now?" she turned to Schneiders.

The secretary looked perplexed for a split second, but then pulled out her smartphone, which seemed to be part of her body anyway, and tapped the screen a few times.

A navigation app, Penny thought. In this modern day and age, it was child's play to find out where you were.

"We just passed Landeck," the assistant announced.

"Should we pull the emergency brake?" asked Louise, addressing no one in particular. "There is an emergency brake on this train, isn't there?"

"Of course, there is," Madeleine replied sharply. "It

just won't help us to stop the train here on the open track. On the contrary." She pointed in the direction of the window, where nothing could be seen except deep black night and swirling snow.

"I know the route," she added. "Shortly after Landeck—that means we're in the middle of nowhere. Not even in good weather could an ambulance drive up to the tracks here." She shook her head. "No way."

Her eyes wandered over to Jacques, who was writhing on the sofa, groaning, then she issued another order to her assistant. "Schneiders, check where the nearest hospital is located."

Nothing in Madeleine's voice let on that one of her sons had just died, and that another one would soon suffer the same fate unless a miracle happened. She kept a cool—no, an ice-cold—head, radiating pure efficiency in a situation in which others would have long since lost theirs. Penny shivered.

Schneiders wiped across the display of her smartphone. "There's a hospital in Zams," she announced, "but that's behind us. "The nearest one is in... oh, well. I'm afraid we're really in the middle of nowhere. I don't even have decent telephone reception here."

"Hurry up, will you!" Madeleine nagged.

"Excuse me, Madame. I'm quite a stranger—"

"—to Austrian geography? Really, Schneiders, I thought I could rely on you."

The assistant winced, but then tapped away on her

phone again. "No reception at all now, I'm afraid," she mumbled. Beads of sweat collected on her forehead.

"St. Anton," said Madeleine, after a short silence. "That should be close by. Just a few miles ahead. It has a decent hospital, if I remember correctly. And I know a very good doctor there. Dr. Ludwig Stiller, a real luminary."

She hesitated only a few seconds, then seemed to have made a decision.

"When can we be there? Well, go ahead, Schneiders, don't stand around, instruct the train driver! Full speed to St. Anton. And call an ambulance. Tell them to come straight to the station. In the meantime, I'll try to reach Dr. Stiller."

Madame Salmann certainly likes to travel to St. Anton for the winter season, thought Penny. The small village on the Arlberg was *the* meeting place for the members of high society when it came to skiing, or simply to spending the winter months among their peers. St. Anton had no shortage of spas, beauty farms, luxury restaurants and bars. Penny's mother regularly liked to spend her winter holidays there.

Schneiders scurried away, Madeleine rummaged through her purse for her own phone, and Penny watched Jacques Salmann undergo the same process of rapid physical deterioration as his brother had barely an hour earlier.

We'll never make it in time. The thought forced itself into Penny's head and could not be dispelled. Jacques will be dead long before he sees the inside of an ambulance. It's happening too fast.

10

St. Anton am Arlberg train station
1:15 am

As the Occident Express pulled into the St. Anton station, Penny could barely see through the panoramic windows and glass roof of the train. A violent storm was howling and swirling dense white snowflakes around as if in a wind tunnel. The lamps on the platform gave only a diffuse light, as though through a fog.

Just beside the track rose a concrete wall that seemed to support the flank of a mountain. The wall was held up by huge bolts, or whatever those things were called when their heads reached twenty centimeters in diameter.

Dr. Ludwig Stiller, the doctor whom Madame Salmann had called, was already waiting on the platform. He was older, bald, and a little roundish, with piercing blue eyes. He was completely wrapped up in warm clothes, but still shivering.

When the door of the train opened and he climbed aboard, he spread heavy wet snow on the stairs. He brought with him a gush of ice-cold air that hit Penny like a whiplash. She had followed right behind Madame Salmann to receive the doctor. Behind her huddled the family members. Those who were still alive.

"The ambulance is going to take a while," Dr. Stiller said in lieu of a greeting. Penny noticed that he didn't even reach out his hand to Madame Salmann. Instead, he rubbed and massaged his fingers, which looked half frozen.

"The roads are all closed," he explained. "Dreadful winter weather all over the state. I only made it this far because I live less than two hundred yards away. And the route already felt like an Everest expedition."

"There is no longer any hurry," Madeleine Salmann said flatly. "My sons are dead. Both of them." Her voice sounded as dispassionate as before, only her lower lip quivering as she spoke.

The doctor closed his eyelids briefly and exhaled. Then he took Madame Salmann's hand after all. "Where are they? Let me see if I can't do something for them at all. What on earth happened, anyway?"

A sigh escaped the old lady—which made her seem almost human for a moment. "I have no idea. Come on. See for yourself. But you won't be able to do anything."

The small group, consisting of Penny, the secretary, and the remaining family members, surrounded the doctor and again crowded into Penny's compartment.

Dr. Stiller stopped when he saw the two dead bodies. Even to a medical layman like Penny there was no doubt that Madeleine was right. Not even the best doctor in the world could have helped the two brothers.

"Good grief," muttered Dr. Stiller, then he composed himself and stepped toward Jacques, who was hanging lifelessly on the sofa. His head had sunk to his chest; one could almost believe he was just taking a little nap, if the rest of his body hadn't cramped grotesquely in death.

"He was bitten," Penny said, because none of the others spoke up. "Or stung. Just like his brother." She pointed to Xavier's body on her bed.

The doctor got down on his knees and studied Jacques' foot in detail, which was grotesquely swollen. As he did so, he mumbled something unintelligible, but it sounded rather astonished. No, completely perplexed.

"Do you think it could have been a poisonous snake?" asked a shaky voice.

Penny turned around. It was Louise, Jacque's fiancée. She was a widow now, even before the wedding. She clung to Erika's arm and looked as if she were about to lose her mind. There was nothing left of her beauty, of the sunny and friendly disposition that had made her shine all evening.

Penny intervened. "It would have to have been a tiny snake. Otherwise we would have noticed it, wouldn't we? And look, Doctor, how close together those two holes are." She pointed her index finger at Jacques' foot.

The doctor nodded.

"I've never heard of a deadly venomous snake that small," Penny continued.

"Neither have I," said Dr. Stiller.

"Then what could it have been?" asked Madeleine, who now seemed to be completely back in control of herself.

"A fatal spider bite, I suppose," the doctor said.

He tilted his head. "Something I've never encountered in my entire career, I must say. It can't be a sting, because then there would just be one hole. They're very close together, but it's clearly *two* related wounds. It wasn't a big animal, if you go by that. But extremely venomous. Death occurred within fifteen minutes, you said?"

Penny nodded her head.

Dr. Stiller had the course of Xavier's death struggle described to him exhaustively. Penny spoke haltingly, careful not to go into too much excruciating detail in front of the family of the deceased, but at the same time providing the doctor with all the information he needed.

"And with his brother here, it went exactly the same way?" asked Dr. Stiller.

"Yes."

"Unbelievable." The doctor rubbed his chin, on which a gray shadow of beard was visible. "In Austria, I definitely don't know of any animal that could do such damage. Although there have been some new arrivals in our country in recent years. Due to climate change, they say. The thorn finger spider, for example. Or the Nosferatu—a hideous palm-sized and very hairy beast," he said, visibly disgusted. "Similar to a tarantula. These are two of the few spiders in Europe that can even bite a human. The common spider native to our country has fangs so weak they can't even penetrate our skin. But if a thorn finger spider or a Nosferatu gets you, that's hardly worse than a wasp sting either."

"An allergic reaction, perhaps?" asked Penny with no real conviction.

The doctor looked skeptical. "Two allergy sufferers at once? And a fatal reaction within minutes?" He shook his head. "The likelihood of that would be—"

He broke off, shrugging his shoulders. "No, that's out of the question. The condition of the deceased also contradicts this hypothesis." He raised his head and looked over at Xavier, whom he had not yet examined closely.

"No," he affirmed. "There's no way this was an allergic reaction. We're dealing with poisoning here. By a highly toxic substance."

Penny's guts tightened. She squinted into the corners of the room, then at the glass ceiling of the compartment, on which a thick layer of snow had accumulated in the meantime. She almost expected to see some vermin out of a horror movie lowering itself from up there at that very moment. The mention of the palm-sized, hairy spider had planted nightmarish images in her head. And the others in the room seemed to feel the same way.

Louise was desperately clinging to Erika's arm, Martin was stepping from one foot to the other—only Madeleine and her assistant still looked reasonably composed, although Schneiders had also pulled in her shoulders and seemed rather intimidated compared to her otherwise-competent demeanor.

"As I said, I'm no expert when it comes to deadly spiders," Dr. Stiller resumed his explanations, "but I don't think there are too many suitable candidates worldwide. If we were in Australia, my guess would be a funnel-web spider. You find those even in the center of Sydney. I think the spacing of the bite holes would be the right size for this species. The male spiders are much smaller than the females, but five times as venomous. And very aggressive, they say. But of course, Australian doctors and hospitals are equipped with the appropriate antivenom."

The doctor looked into the faces of those present, one by one. "I don't suppose any of you have seen anything creepy-crawly on the train since you left Vienna. Or maybe cobwebs?"

Madeleine wrinkled her nose. Penny could literally read her mind. *Cobwebs on my luxury train.* Every surface in the Occident Express, every corner, no matter how dark, literally shone with cleanliness.

"How would a spider like that have gotten on board?" Penny turned to the doctor. "It couldn't survive in our climate this time of year, could it?"

"Certainly not," the doctor said. "Perhaps it was brought in with some tropical fruit for the galley. Such incidents are not unheard of. That's the only explanation I can come up with. But even that seems very unlikely. "

11

Madeleine took a step forward. She looked over at Jacques again, then at Xavier on the bed, but then tore herself away from the sight of her dead sons and fixed her gaze on Schneiders. "Tell the train driver to move on. There's nothing more I can do for my boys anyway—except to bury them at home with dignity. And the passengers must not find out about this incident, is that understood? A poisonous spider aboard the Occident Express..." She closed her eyes and exhaled audibly.

Schneiders wanted to hurry away to comply with her boss's order, but the doctor stepped in her way. "Wait," he said. "This isn't as easy as you might think."

Madeleine looked at him with raised eyebrows. She was clearly not used to anyone questioning her orders.

"We have two unexplained deaths here," the doctor said. "We need to notify the police."

"Unexplained? But you just told to us that—"

The doctor interrupted her: "I was merely making suppositions. As I said, I'm not an expert on poisonous animals. And these two deaths are beyond anything I've ever encountered in my career. A thorough autopsy needs to be done so we can find out what really killed your sons."

"The police?" echoed Madeleine. "How do you imagine that? My passengers—"

Again, the doctor interrupted her. "Madeleine," he said insistently, as if he were trying to coax an old friend. "These are the regulations we must follow. You can't just go on. And don't you want to know what killed your sons?"

Madeleine clenched her teeth. Her eyes narrowed to dark slits. She muttered something that Penny couldn't understand, but that sounded an awful lot like a curse; anything but ladylike.

Then the old matriarch turned to Schneiders again, keeping her eyes on the doctor as well. "I'll tell you what we'll do. You, Schneiders, talk to the train conductor. Inform the passengers that we're stuck here for a while. Make up some story about the snow drifts. An avalanche on the track ahead. A technical failure due to the storm, I don't know. That's still better than two dead people—who fell victim to some killer spider. On board my train! "

She then turned to Penny with a jerk. "What do you advise, how should we proceed?" she asked.

"Me?" said Penny in amazement.

"You are a detective, you told me. Aren't you? Now you can prove yourself. Find out what killed my sons. Especially since they died in *your* compartment."

Penny swallowed. The accusation that resonated in these words could not be ignored. Fortunately, the matriarch did not inquire why Xavier had been in Penny's cabin in the first place. But the champagne bottle and two glasses probably spoke for themselves.

A nasty thought went through Penny's mind: what if the deadly vermin had struck later? At a time when Xavier and she... well, had already been together under the covers? What if Xavier had died in the middle of making love? Or even worse, what if the critter had chosen *her* as its victim? She didn't even want to think about that possibility.

"If it really was a poisonous spider that killed your sons," she turned back to Madeleine, "it must still be on board. It would hardly have crawled out into the blizzard voluntarily, even if it had found a suitable crack or other way out of the train. "

"There are no cracks here, as you put it, my dear," Madeleine said indignantly.

"Yes, uh, of course. As I said, the critter must still be on board. I suggest we do a thorough search of every corner. Starting with my compartment here. We must proceed very carefully, of course, so as not to let anyone else get bitten."

Madeleine didn't reply—which Penny took as agreement. So she continued: "We'll split up. Everyone searches their own compartment, and if train crews are dispensable, they can check the corridors. There is hardly any shelter for a critter there anyway, so it can be done quickly. If we don't find anything here in the two front carriages, then we'll search the lounge car. I think most of the passengers will already have gone to bed at this hour. And let's also hope the spider hasn't reached the restaurant. Or even the rear carriages. If this critter exists at all."

She glanced at her wristwatch. 2:05 a.m.

Erika took a step back and gave her husband a strange look. Neither seemed very taken with the idea of rummaging through the train in search of a deadly insect. Penny couldn't blame them.

She herself felt nauseous at the idea of possibly encountering a creepy, hairy spider the size of a human hand somewhere. Even if the doctor had claimed that the animal must be quite small. Maybe it was huge and only had fangs that stood close together.

Louise was no longer crying. She was leaning against the wall right next to the door and seemed to have lapsed into a kind of lethargic rigidity. But at least she now raised her head, looked at Penny out of reddened eyes, and nodded. "I'll check our compartment," she said mechanically.

"I must protest!" the doctor spoke up. "What you're suggesting, this search operation; it's far too dangerous! Do you want to risk someone else getting bitten? I really think we should—"

"We'll be careful," Madeleine interrupted him, in a tone that nipped any contradiction in the bud. "The best thing is for everyone to put on their winter boots before we start searching. Then our feet will be protected. And otherwise, we all have eyes in our heads, don't we? We now know where the danger is coming from."

She didn't ask if any of those present had even brought a pair of winter boots on board, or if anyone preferred not to take part in the search operation. Her word was command; objections were not tolerated; the reputation of her luxury train took precedence over personal interests. End of discussion.

Penny felt guilty because she herself had suggested the search operation for the spider. She realized that the doctor was right. The critter *was* dangerous, but still her detective instincts and her curiosity, which she could hardly ever keep in check, won out in the end. As much as she was afraid of creepy-crawlies, her urge to solve the two deaths was stronger. After all, she was a budding detective!

Dr. Stiller made one more attempt to bring Madeleine to her senses, which she stifled with an imperious wave of her hand. Then he admitted defeat. He just groaned softly and said, "But you yourself should definitely lie down for a while, Madeleine. Think of your heart! I can give you a sedative if you like. "

She dismissed it. "I don't need anything. The reputation of my beloved train is at stake now. Which, you may recall, is dedicated to the memory of my late husband. I will search my own compartment together with Schneiders. Then hers. We will do our part. "

The doctor nodded slowly. "But for heaven's sake be careful, don't reach anywhere you can't see! And don't forget to keep an eye on the walls and ceiling."

Penny looked around her compartment. This was where the two men had died. It was a crime scene. During the search, it would be important to not destroy any clues, in case they couldn't track down the spider, and ended up with two unexplained deaths after all.

She groaned inwardly. The crime scene had long since been contaminated. Any number of people had been running around in here for several hours. The dead had been touched, as had the majority of the surfaces in the suite. If a forensics team needed to be called in after all, they would not be happy.

"Will you stay on board, doctor?" Penny asked. *In case there is another emergency,* she added in her mind, but did not voice her concern. That would only frighten the others even more.

Dr. Stiller, however, seemed to understand.

"Of course," he said thoughtfully. "But please, as I said, use extreme caution. We have no antidote available here for this spider, whatever species it may ultimately belong to."

That means, if someone else gets bitten, even the doctor can do nothing but watch them die, Penny thought.

A great prospect. Wouldn't it be better to evacuate the entire train after all? And try to accommodate the passengers in the nearest hotels, even if that was certainly not an easy undertaking in the middle of this snowstorm. But then what—call an exterminator?

No, Penny told herself. First, they had to find out what they were really dealing with. Maybe they had overlooked something or had started from the wrong premise. The theory of an imported killer spider from faraway lands that attacked two people in one evening seemed just too farfetched the longer she thought about it. Outside of horror films, even the most poisonous animals didn't just pounce on harmless people for no reason at all. Or did they?

Neither Xavier nor Jacques had stepped on the critter. It had to have climbed onto their feet of its own free will—and then had it bitten them completely unprovoked?

Plus, did even the deadliest spider have enough venom to kill more than one person in a row? Penny made a mental note to research this point as soon as she found the time.

But if this beast did exist after all, the passengers here in the front carriages—Madame Salmann's family—were now warned and on guard, and the hypothetical monster certainly wouldn't crawl all the way through the lounge and restaurant cars to the rear of the train.

"What about the police?" the doctor intervened again.

"If we do find this spider, we won't have any more unexplained deaths," Madeleine replied before Penny could say anything. "Then I guess we don't need the police, do we? Don't you realize, Ludwig, how this will look to my passengers if police officers suddenly invade my train?"

"Yes, but—" the doctor wanted to object.

"What if we aren't able to find a spider?" Penny chimed in.

"In that case we can still call the police," Madeleine said tersely. She didn't give the doctor any chance for further objections. Instead, she turned to the members of her family.

"What are you waiting for? Let's find this vermin!" she ordered in the imperious tone of a general.

The others started moving like sleepwalkers. Their faces were marked with perplexity and fear.

Penny stopped Madeleine, who was also heading for the door, and whispered to her: "Madame Salmann, please make sure no one can leave the train for the time being. Ask the conductor to keep the outer doors closed. And we'll seal off my compartment, too, after I've searched it. We leave the dead where they are. And we'll make sure no one gets into the front cars from behind."

"What's the point of all this?" asked Madame Salmann suspiciously.

"Just a precaution... in case it wasn't a spider that killed your sons after all," Penny replied.

12

"I think this spider is a phantom," Penny told Dr. Stiller. She settled into the chair in front of the fine wooden desk and took a few deep breaths.

There were no other seats available in her compartment, because the body of Jacques Salmann still lay on the sofa and that of Xavier occupied the bed. Penny avoided looking at either of them. After the doctor's examination, no one had touched the dead—just in case a police investigation would be necessary in the end.

"The others probably haven't discovered anything either," Dr. Stiller replied. "Otherwise, I'm sure they would have let us know."

The doctor had helped Penny search her compartment—which was, after all, the spider's most likely location. If the mysterious animal existed at all.

Now, however, Dr. Stiller also admitted defeat. He looked wordlessly at Penny and made a puzzled expression.

Penny frowned. While she had carefully searched through her narrow closet, which contained only a few of her clothes, a new thought had occurred to her. One that hadn't given her a moment's peace since—

71

which was why she now decided to share it with the doctor.

"What if we can't find the spider because it was disposed of long ago?" she asked.

Dr. Stiller eyed her quizzically. "I don't believe they would have just flushed the vermin down the toilet if it had been found. I thought we made it clear how important it was that it be correctly identified. We certainly would have been informed."

"That's not what I'm getting at," Penny said. She hesitated, but then quickly continued speaking. "What if this spider didn't get on the train with some tropical fruit, but was deliberately introduced?"

"I'm afraid I don't understand."

"What if someone brought it on board—with the deliberate intention of letting it do its deadly work on the train? Someone who got rid of it after the deed was done? After all, they could have just flushed the critter down the toilet, as you just noted. A wonderfully simple way to get rid of something so small. Wouldn't that be the perfect weapon: one that you can make disappear, never to be seen again, when you no longer need it?"

The doctor raised both eyebrows. "Are you talking about... murder?" he asked incredulously. "By poisonous spider?"

Penny shrugged her shoulders. "I know how crazy that sounds. But it's possible, isn't it? It seems at least more likely to me than such a monster straying all by itself from the other side of the world to Austria of all places. In the middle of December, and onto a train no less? A train which is kept meticulously clean? And once on board this critter starts attacking people indiscriminately? It's not a new idea to put a poisonous snake in an enemy's bed or something similar. A scorpion into a shoe... It's all been done before. So why not put a killer insect on a train?"

The doctor frowned. "My dear young lady—" He interrupted himself. "Madeleine mentioned that you were a detective?"

"Aspiring detective," Penny corrected him, but he didn't seem to hear her. He was already going on, "First, spiders are not insects, they are arachnids. They have eight legs—versus six in insects."

"Thanks for the tutoring," Penny said. "Does it really matter? I—"

"And second," the doctor interrupted her, "you should be careful that your imagination—which is undoubtedly very active—doesn't get the better of you. The kind of assassination you are imagining would be very... how shall I put it?"

"Very unusual? Highly unorthodox?" asked Penny. "I'm quite aware of that. After all, it's just a possibility that has crossed my mind. I just wanted to get your opinion on it."

"My opinion? I firmly believe that poisonous spiders wouldn't work as murder weapons. That is, outside of television crime shows. Think about it, how should this have happened? The animal was *not* hidden in a shoe or something similar in the expectation that the potential victim would step on it. So in our case, the perpetrator would need to drop the spider directly on the foot of his victim, and even then there would be no guarantee the animal would actually bite, instead of simply crawling away, which would be the critter's natural reaction. Venomous animals generally only use their weapons for hunting or defense."

Penny nodded. "I'm aware of that."

"You were alone in the compartment with the first victim when he was bitten, weren't you? There was no potential perpetrator around, if I understood you correctly? No one who could have sicced a spider on Mr. Salmann."

"Yeah, I get it."

"There you go!" said the doctor. "And even if we were to consider such a scenario: is this unknown person supposed to have trained the critter to be a killer? Make it pounce on its victim on command and bite?"

Penny silently shook her head.

"See my point? So put that crazy theory right out of your mind, my dear child! "

"Okay," Penny said meekly, but she was not fully convinced.

The spider was in your compartment, a warning voice said in the back of her head. If the beast had really been placed there on purpose, that would mean... that someone was targeting *you*! Not Xavier, who was only a guest in your suite, and quite a spontaneous one at that.

Oh my goodness. She couldn't stop her brain from running amok. Who had known she would be on the Occident Express tonight? Her mother, of course. And her fiancé. The two people who had broken up with her since she had decided to train as a detective. But neither of them would go so far as to unleash a poisonous spider on her, hopefully—or would they?

Stefan, her fiancé—no, her ex-fiancé—certainly sometimes had problems controlling his temper. You could call him a hothead. But an assassin?

She did not get any further with this frightening thought, because at that moment there was a knock at the door. Several knocks in a row, to be exact, and very brisk ones.

Penny stood up and hurried across the compartment, still letting her eyes wander over the walls and ceiling, half expecting a monster spider to materialize there. With a jerk, she opened the door—and found herself face to face with Christiane Schneiders.

Madame Salmann's assistant glanced around the room, nodded briefly at the doctor, then tilted her head close to Penny's ear. "May I have a word with you, Ms. Küfer?"

She didn't wait for an answer, but gently grabbed Penny by the sleeve and pulled her out into the corridor. "Madame Salmann sent me. She wants to see you urgently," she whispered. "Up front, in her suite.

Would you come with me, please?"

"What is this about?" asked Penny. Schneiders's secretive manner suggested that she had not come because Madame Salmann had discovered the spider.

The assistant hesitated. She looked around suspiciously, but the corridor was completely deserted.

"We can count on your discretion, can't we?" she asked then, still in a whisper. "As a detective... you have a duty of confidentiality to your clients, right?"

Penny refrained from informing the woman that she had just begun training as a detective. She had tried to explain this to Dr. Stiller just before, but apparently no one cared.

Madame Salmann, however, had to know; at dinner with the old lady, Penny had talked in great detail about her training at the detective academy and about her career aspirations.

And yet the matriarch wanted to speak to Penny in her professional capacity?

"Don't worry, I'm a hundred percent discreet," she answered Schneiders. "But tell me, now—what's going on?"

The assistant seemed to be at a loss for the right words. "Madame wouldn't tell me, she just... gave some hints."

She moved even closer so that her lips almost touched Penny's ear. "I think Madame believes her sons were murdered. Oh please, come and talk to her," she added. "Madame is beside herself."

Schneiders peered into Penny's compartment, where the doctor was standing by the window, looking out into the snowstorm. He probably wanted to avoid seeming curious and had turned away after Schneiders had pulled Penny out into the corridor.

The assistant made a head movement toward the doctor. "I asked Madame to send for Monsieur Stiller, too, because she was very upset. But she wouldn't hear of it. She is a very strong woman, but she is old, isn't she? It could be dangerous, I'm afraid, if she doesn't want to take anything to calm her down!"

The assistant's face showed great concern.

"She wants to talk to you alone, Ms. Küfer," she then repeated, this time a little louder and seemingly halfway back to her usual very composed self. "Please come with me."

Penny hesitated no longer, but followed the assistant down the corridor. Under all the glass in the outer shell of the train, one had the impression of walking through a snow tunnel.

Murdered?—Penny tried to process the information Schneiders had just given her. The matriarch thought her two sons had been murdered? Was she following a thought process similar to what Penny had just gone over with the doctor?

Schneiders moved forward briskly, but Penny had no trouble following her. Now that the train was at a standstill there was no need to worry about keeping her balance in a tight curve.

They passed through the airlock that stood between Penny's carriage and the one in which the owner's suite was located. Madame Salmann had chosen to occupy the foremost cabin in her luxury train.

They had only gone halfway across the car when the door of Madeleine's compartment flew open, and a woman rushed out. She was screaming loudly.

It was Erika Salmann. Her eyes wide with horror, she ran toward Penny and the assistant. She almost tripped over her own feet.

"Madeleine is dead!" she cried in a choked voice. "She's been murdered!"

13

Penny managed to stop the completely hysterical woman in her tracks. She got hold of Erika Salmann's shoulder and gently pushed her back into Madeleine's compartment from which she had just rushed out.

Schneiders entered the suite behind them, but stopped right on the doorstep as if struck by lightning. Tears welled up in her eyes when she saw the body of her employer.

Madeleine was slumped at her desk. And Erika had spoken the truth—the old lady was dead; there could be no doubt about that.

Penny had trouble processing the sight that met her eyes. Madeleine's upper body had fallen forward on the desk top, her head turned to the side and resting on her right arm—as if the old lady had been overcome by an urgent need to sleep in the middle of her work.

However, it was plain to see that Madeleine was not asleep: the handle of a knife protruded from the base of her neck, just above her left shoulder, and the silk robe the old lady was wearing had soaked up so much blood that it glistened a bright scarlet. Madeleine's eyes were clouded and stared blankly into space.

Penny approached the lifeless woman, and gently grasped her wrist. She could no longer feel a pulse. She bent down, close to the old lady's face, but there was no sign of breathing either.

And yet, Penny told herself, she had to fetch Dr. Stiller immediately. Maybe he could work some kind of medical miracle after all.

She turned to Schneiders, "You and Erika stay here, and I'll get the doctor, okay?"

Schneiders nodded, but seemed to stare right through Penny's head. Her gaze was still fixed on Madeleine's body.

All that blood.

I have to get these two women out of here as quickly as possible, Penny thought. It would only increase the shock they had suffered if they were exposed to this sight any longer.

Nonetheless, the doctor had priority. "Stay where you are," Penny repeated and once again sought the assistant's gaze, but again reaped no more than a mechanical nod.

"You must not touch anything or let anyone in, okay?"

"Right," Schneiders replied flatly.

Penny scurried out of the cabin and ran down the aisle. It took her barely a minute to reach her own compartment in the next car.

"What's wrong?" Dr. Stiller exclaimed as soon as she stormed into the suite. He could probably tell from the look on her face that something terrible had happened.

"Come with me, please," was all Penny managed to say. The doctor wouldn't be able to save Madeleine's life; she was sure of that, but she still felt it was her duty to get him to her as soon as possible.

The doctor followed her without further questions.

When he entered Madeleine's compartment and saw the body in front of him, he recoiled as if he had run into an invisible wall.

"Jesus," he gasped, but then he seemed to remember his medical duty and quickly crossed the suite.

Schneiders and Erika had not moved at all, it seemed. Schneiders was leaning against the wall, right next to the door, but seemed to have herself halfway under control again. At least she looked at Penny and the doctor out of eyes that were very red, but otherwise seemed almost normal again.

Erika, on the other hand, still sat on the sofa where she had collapsed earlier, as soon as Penny had let go of her. She didn't move, looking as limp as a discarded doll. Her eyes were teary.

The doctor bent over Madeleine and performed some routine-looking movements. Penny could not see what exactly he was doing, because his body completely blocked the view of the dead woman. Was he checking for pulse and breath, as she herself had amateurishly tried to do?

After a minute at most, Dr. Stiller straightened up

and turned to Penny. He shook his head wordlessly but meaningfully, and thus confirmed what she had already suspected: no doctor in the world could help Madeleine Salmann anymore.

Dr. Stiller exhaled heavily. "I'll notify the police immediately," he said. "I know the officers at the local station."

Penny nodded in agreement. There was no way to avoid the police now. The search for an ominous poisonous spider had suddenly turned into a murder case.

The doctor was already speaking into his cell phone. He seemed to be talking to a man he knew well. They were on a first-name basis, and the doctor's statement was apparently not questioned, however insane it might have sounded to the police officer on the other end of the line.

Dr. Stiller didn't have to repeat anything, and hung up the next moment. "They'll be on their way as soon as possible," he told Penny. "But it's going to take a while. They have a major traffic accident on their hands with several people injured; the roads are blocked by tons of snow; one of their emergency vehicles broke down.... What do I know? I'm not sure I got everything right. Telephone reception was abominable."

He scratched his head, looking like he could use some medical attention himself.

"Major Crimes will also be notified," he added. "The

officer I spoke to will take care of that. It may take longer for them to arrive, though. I don't know if they'll even get through, given the weather conditions."

He looked out of the window, where hardly anything was visible anymore, due to the heavy snowfall. Then he turned to Penny, seemingly abandoning all hope of any help from the outside.

"What do we do now?" he asked.

She swallowed hard—so it was up to her. The first few minutes after a crime was committed could be crucial when it came to finding the culprit; that much she knew. And they would be on their own on this train for a good while longer.

First and foremost, it probably made sense to secure the crime scene and ascertain the most important facts. And she was the only one on this train who was capable of doing that. No doubt about it.

She had at least a basic knowledge of criminal investigation, albeit of a purely theoretical nature. She had had nothing more than a week of basic detective training to show for it—where they had mainly focused on legal and bureaucratic matters. They had certainly not covered investigating a crime or securing a murder scene.

Additionally, she had read quite a few textbooks... and all in all that was still more than the other passengers could bring to the table. Plus, she had been fantasizing about solving crimes all her life—even if she'd never have dreamt of anything even close to what she'd experienced tonight on this train. She had to keep a cool head and take charge until the police officers arrived.

Penny forced herself to take a closer look at the fatal wound on Madeleine's neck, even though the smell of blood rose to her nostrils and made her nauseous.

She looked at the weapon, whose striking handle of dark precious wood, decorated with the Occident Express's logo, she recognized.

"A steak knife from the restaurant," she told Dr. Stiller. "That could have been procured by just about anyone."

The doctor nodded, but said nothing.

Penny turned to Erika, who was still reclining on the sofa, looking very pale. "What were you doing here with your mother-in-law?" she asked her.

"I... I didn't kill her!" Erika blurted out. "You don't think I could—" Her voice broke.

"It's okay," Penny said quickly. "Don't worry, I'm not accusing you of anything. I just want to know what happened here."

Erika nodded vigorously a few times, but did not utter another word.

Penny walked over to her, and put her hand on her arm to reassure her.

The doctor seemed to realize only now that there were people in the room who needed his help. He jerked into motion, heaved the small doctor's bag he had brought with him onto the bed and opened it. He was probably looking for a sedative to give to Erika.

The small but sturdily built woman's breathing was irregular. But finally, after Dr. Stiller had given her a shot in the arm, she was able to come up with a reasonably clear report.

"Madeleine called me on the phone," she told Penny as she twirled a strand of her short, somewhat bristly brown hair between her fingers. "But I wasn't quick enough. I was just in the bathroom and when I finally picked up, Madeleine had already hung up. I called back right away, but no one answered. So, I came over in person. I was already done with our compartment. With the search, I mean. For the critter."

She pointed at the dead old lady with an awkward hand gesture. "But she wasn't killed by a spider," she whispered. New tears sprang up in the corners of her eyes.

Penny turned to the assistant. "Schneiders, when you left your boss earlier and came to my compartment to fetch me—did you run into anyone along the way?"

The question was obvious. After all, the killer could only have reached Madeleine's compartment through the corridor. The outside doors of the train had been locked, as Penny had suggested a while ago, so there was no other way there.

Schneiders shook her head. "Not a soul," she said.

"No steward or waiter either?"

"No." The assistant audibly sucked in a breath, then

85

her voice sounded a bit more firm again.

"Certainly not," she affirmed. "One of the robo-stewards went past me. Heading for the very front of the train, I think. There's a service compartment for the staff there. And, of course, the driver's booth."

"Delivering a little refreshment for the staff?" asked Penny.

"Possibly. I wasn't paying attention to what the robo-steward was carrying."

Well, the robot is unlikely to have stabbed Madame Salmann, Penny told herself.

Schneiders detached herself from the wall and took a step toward Penny. Her knees still seemed a little weak, but otherwise she looked as if she had mostly regained her composure. She avoided looking in the direction of the dead body, however.

"When you left your boss," Penny continued, "what was she busy doing?"

"She was sitting at her desk, like she is now," Schneiders replied.

"With her back to the door?"

"No, she had turned around to talk to me—when she told me to fetch you."

After that, the old lady could have turned back to her work at the desk, Penny figured. To the right of the body lay a thin tablet computer that must have gone into sleep mode. The screen was black.

To all appearances, the murderer had crept up be-hind Madeleine and killed her with a well-aimed stab to the neck. Presumably before she had even noticed his presence.

The steak knives from the restaurant were perfectly-sharpened instruments. Penny had been able to see that for herself at dinner. You didn't need to be an expert to kill your victim with such a weapon.

She turned to Schneiders again: "You came straight to my compartment, I suppose? Or did you enter one of the other suites on the way?"

"I came straight to you. Madame wanted to see you urgently. I told you so." Schneiders was almost back to her old self now; the efficient, somewhat brittle assistant Penny had met in the evening.

"So you were only gone a few minutes?" Penny was thinking out loud.

"Right."

"And you didn't meet anyone on the way, you say. Did you see anyone in the compartments? Were there any doors open?"

"I wasn't paying attention," Schneiders said. "I went to you as fast as I could."

"Okay," Penny said. "Thanks."

The assistant nodded, walked the few steps over to the sofa and settled down next to Madeleine's daughter-in-law, who now had her head buried in her hands but otherwise was sitting motionless.

The doctor also offered Schneiders a sedative, but she refused with a quick wave of her hand.

"I'm going to check on the other family members for

a minute," Penny announced. "I'll be right back. Okay?"

"All right," Dr. Stiller said. He seemed to be well back in control now, but still glad that Penny had taken the lead.

14

Penny left the dead matriarch's compartment and walked down the aisle. She'd decided to ask the members of the family to stay in their suites for now. It was not a good idea to let more people trample around Madeleine's compartment—the scene of the crime.

Observe carefully, Penny! she admonished herself. She was now clearly dealing with a murder case. Every little detail could be important; every lead, every clue. It was now a matter of observing as attentively as possible.

She wished—not for the first time tonight—to have come much further already with her training. Then she would have been better equipped for the current situation. As it was, however, she had no choice but to rely on her instincts and the little knowledge she had acquired from books.

The corridor lay deserted. The first cabin door she passed was locked. This was not surprising, because this compartment belonged to Schneiders, whose accommodation was right next to her boss's.

The next compartment door, on the other hand, stood ajar. Penny paused and peered inside. As far as she could see, the suite was empty. Martin and Erika

89

Salmann had taken up quarters here for the trip—she had known that since the large-scale search for the spider. Penny also knew Erika's whereabouts right now, but where had Martin gone?

She ran on, and crossed the airlock to the next carriage, her own. The first compartment here had belonged to Jacques Salmann, who now lay dead in Penny's own suite. And here, too, the door was not locked. Cautiously, she opened it and squinted into the room.

Sitting on the sofa was Louise—almost a mirror image of Erika a few suites away. She too had her head buried in her hands and didn't seem to notice Penny.

Penny gently knocked on the already open door to make her presence known.

Louise startled, but immediately relaxed again when she caught sight of Penny. She hunched her shoulders, which suddenly no longer looked slender and well-proportioned, but downright bony. Almost as if she had lost a few kilos in weight with the loss of her fiancé.

"I found nothing," she said, "No spider anywhere. Not even a housefly." Her voice sounded rough and brittle.

"It's fine," Penny replied. "Please stay in your cabin until I get back to you, okay? Why don't you get some rest?" She gestured with her head toward the bed.

Louise nodded, but did not move from her spot.

Penny closed the door of the compartment and

walked on.

The last suite before hers belonged to Xavier Salmann. The door of this compartment stood wide open, and Martin Salmann was busy on his knees circling the bed and searching the narrow gap underneath. Probably still on the hunt for the spider.

He glanced up at Penny briefly, but then immediately turned his attention back to the floor.

There was at most a hand's width of space under the queen size beds in the compartments. But that was more than enough for a spider, even if it was far larger than the doctor had assumed. Penny had also already scanned this potential hiding place in her compartment—with the help of the flashlight built into her cell phone.

Martin had apparently not come up with this latter idea. He was staring into the darkness under the bed without a light source.

Was she supposed to inform him about his mother's death right now? About his mother's *murder,* to be precise?

No, she decided. Madeleine's eldest son could well have been the assassin himself, even if his charisma was more that of an assistant bookkeeper than of a stone-cold killer. One could be mistaken about people; sometimes very much so.

Dr. Stiller was the only one who, in Penny's eyes, had an airtight alibi for Madeleine's murder. For he had been right with her, in her suite, when the crime had been committed. All the other passengers were now suspects. Martin, Erika and Louise. And Schneiders, too! The faithful assistant must not be ignored. Schneiders could have murdered her boss in cold blood, and then come to Penny with the story that Madeleine wanted to speak to her urgently.

However, the assistant had no apparent motive. She was only an employee, not a family member, and to all appearances she had enjoyed working for her boss. The sons, on the other hand, had detested their mother—and vice versa. But two of them were dead themselves. Only Martin, the eldest, was still alive.

From behind—from the direction of the lounge car, the restaurant, or the other passenger cars—no one could have made it to Madeleine's suite. Schneiders would have encountered such an intruder on the way to Penny's compartment when Madeleine had sent her off on her errand.

Only one of the people who were in the front two cars could have used the brief moment Schneiders had spent with Penny to sneak up to Madeleine, murder her, and quickly disappear back into one of the compartments close by. A high-risk endeavor. Schneiders had asked Penny to come out into the corridor and talk to her there, in order to prevent the doctor from overhearing.

Of course, at this point neither of them had paid attention to whether anyone had left their compartment further forward in the carriage. But still: the murderer must have been lying in wait in the first carriage, near Madeleine's cabin, otherwise they would inevitably have noticed him. Wouldn't they? And he had to have struck at lightning speed after Schneiders had moved away. The risk of being discovered had been enormously high.

But we did spot someone who was with Madeleine, Penny thought. *Erika.* She had stormed out of the matriarch's compartment, practically running into Penny. Was she the murderer who had failed to get away quickly enough from the scene of her bloody deed?

Penny took a step toward Martin in his suite and addressed him. "There's been a new development," she said, trying hard not to let her uncertainty show. "Would you please stay here in your cabin until I return?"

Martin rose and eyed her suspiciously. "What's the matter? Have you found the spider?"

"Not yet," Penny replied. She didn't want to get into a discussion now; she had to use the time until the police arrived to be able to provide the officers with useful information. If she wanted to help solve the case—which she was determined to do.

"I'll be back soon," was all she said. "Please don't leave the compartment." She didn't wait for any further reply, but stepped back out into the corridor and closed the door behind her.

Then she returned at a run to Madeleine's compartment and turned to Schneiders there. She told the assistant to go back to her own cabin, right next door, and stay there.

Schneiders nodded dutifully. "Isn't there anything else I can do?" she asked.

"Not at the moment, thank you."

Schneiders hesitated, but then she nodded again. "Madame trusted you," she said. "She wanted to call you in regarding the death of her sons. She thought you were a very capable young lady. I realized that at dinner. I've rarely seen Madame make a job offer to someone so spontaneously. And she was an excellent judge of character. So I'm going to trust you just as much. I hope you can help the police find whoever did this to her." She stared at her employer's dead body with a scowl.

"Thank you," was all Penny said, though she couldn't deny how pleased she was by the compliment.

Schneiders pulled away and Penny now asked Erika to follow her. "I'm going to walk you back to your compartment, okay?" she said. "Get some rest, and then the doctor will check on you again later."

She glanced sideways at the doctor. He looked at her questioningly, but then nodded. "Yes, of course. No problem."

They all left Madeleine's suite together; Schneiders and Erika disappeared into their compartments, then Penny turned to the doctor. The two of them now stood alone in the corridor. Where could they talk without possibly being overheard? Would the different witnesses, or rather suspects, obey Penny's request and remain dutifully in their suites?

"Let's go into the airlock between the two carriages," she said to the doctor. "There we can keep an eye on the doors of all the cabins, and if we speak quietly, we shouldn't be overheard."

The doctor put his hand on her arm. "You're doing very well," he said. "I think it's admirable... the cool head you're keeping."

Penny's head felt anything but cool. But still, she was a budding detective. That was the purpose of her training. Even if she'd never imagined in her wildest dreams that she would one day have to secure the scene of a murder for the police. But here she was— this was her chance and she was determined not to make any mistakes.

Was there any law that prohibited her from taking over this case until the police arrived? If there were, she was not aware of it. Ignorance did not protect from punishment, at least that much she knew, but no matter. She would do such a good job that the detectives would be grateful to her rather than prosecute her in any way.

"Why did you send the two women to their cabins one by one?" the doctor asked her when they reached the airlock. "I'm sure they would handle the situation better together, if you want my advice."

"I want to isolate the witnesses," Penny explained.

"Or the suspects. However you take it."

That sounded very expert, but she hadn't gotten as far as really knowing what she was talking about in her course. She had picked up the idea of isolating suspects from reading detective novels. The police, when they finally arrived, were supposed to be able to interrogate everyone present individually, without giving them the opportunity to confer with each other beforehand.

The doctor nodded, but did not seem fully convinced. "And what do you want to do now?" he asked.

15

That was a very good question.

Penny considered. "Let's start with Erika Salmann," she finally said. "She came storming out of the murdered woman's cabin toward me. Seemingly in complete shock, but that could have been an act. She claimed that Madame Salmann had called her on the phone. We'll have to check that."

"I understand," the doctor said.

"Hold the fort here for a moment, please? Keep an eye on the doors. I'll see if I can find Madame Salmann's cell phone. Then we can take a look and see if the call really happened." Penny scurried away, back to the murdered woman's compartment.

I'll probably need Schneiders, she thought as she walked down the hall. Hopefully she knows the code to unlock her boss's cell phone.

But when she reached Madeleine's suite and found the cell phone there on the narrow shelf next to the sofa, she realized that the device was unsecured. Very careless, but helpful for her.

She scrolled through the call log and realized that Erika had been telling the truth. Shortly before three in the morning, just a few minutes before Madeleine had been murdered, the old lady had dialed a mobile number. Immediately afterwards, a call had been returned from the same number, but it had gone unanswered.

Penny put the phone back, walked two doors down, and stuck her head into the compartment where she had left Erika earlier.

Martin's wife was sitting on the bed staring unblinkingly at Penny when she entered.

"Would you please tell me your phone number?" Penny asked straight out. There was no time for long explanations now.

Fortunately, Erika didn't seem surprised by the question; she readily gave the exact number that had registered in Madeleine's call list.

Penny thanked her, then left again, running back in the direction from which she had just come. She looked out through the aisle windows into the night. The platform, of which only a few meters were visible at all, lay buried under a thick blanket of snow, although it was actually covered by a narrow roof.

The storm must have blown in these white masses, and it raged and howled unabated. Was there any chance at all that the local police would get through to them soon? Not to mention the specialists from the criminal investigation department, who had to make a much longer journey.

She returned to Dr. Stiller in the airlock. "The telephone call... I was able to verify it," she explained to him.

He nodded wordlessly. "Why do you think Madeleine wanted to see her daughter-in-law?" he then asked.

"She might have thought Erika had something to do with the deaths of Jacques and Xavier," Penny replied. "To me, that would be the most obvious explanation."

"You think she was going to confront Erika?"

"Possibly. And when Erika didn't answer the call, Madeleine sent her assistant to discuss her suspicions with me. While Erika took the opportunity to sneak into Madeleine's compartment and silence her forever."

The doctor raised his eyebrows. "But that's crazy," he exclaimed.

"Of course it is, doctor. I am fully aware of how far-fetched it all sounds. But nevertheless, our murderer can only be one of four people: Erika, Martin, Louise or Schneiders. We'll have to get used to this idea, whether we like it or not."

The doctor shook his head in disbelief. "Impossible," he whispered, rubbing his bald head.

"There's something about this knife that bothers me," Penny continued. "I mean, if Erika—or anyone else—decided on the spur of the moment to kill Madeleine, they didn't have time to run into the restaurant car first and grab a knife."

"They could have already taken it at dinner, couldn't they?" the doctor replied.

"But how did they know they would need it later? The other two murders were committed with the help of the poisonous spider. That was the preferred weapon of our murderer. So why steal a knife at dinner?"

The doctor gave a little cough. "The other two murders? But I've already told you that's impossible! One cannot commit a murder by poisonous spider, my word on it! At least not the way it happened with Xavier. He was all alone with you. Nobody could have put that critter on his flipping foot!"

"Madeleine, however, expressed that very suspicion to Schneiders," Penny insisted. "That her sons were murdered. That's why she wanted to see me. She must have assumed that her sons' deaths had not been an accident. And she *must* have been right in her apprehension. Otherwise she wouldn't have been murdered, would she? She must have seen or heard something, and the murderer picked up on it. He—or she—seized their first opportunity, when Schneiders left the cabin. He acted immediately, at the highest risk, to silence Madeleine. So we can be sure that the death of the two brothers was not a tragic accident. We must accept that as a fact, incredible as it may sound."

"I see what you mean," Dr. Stiller said. "But still, an assassination with a trained spider that attacked on command? How in the world did you imagine that? Aside from the fact that we haven't found any trace of the animal. "

"I have no idea," Penny said. "Maybe the intended victims were inconspicuously contaminated with some attractant? And the spider then merely had to be released near them? Then, after the deed was done, it returned to its master, and he made it disappear. Down the toilet. We've been through this before."

The scenario she was imagining sounded like something out of a James Bond movie. Penny had to admit that much to herself.

Had she gotten onto the wrong track? Were Jacques and Xavier just random victims who had simply had the bad luck that a venomous animal had chosen them, of all people? Perhaps the killer had simply released the animal on the train and trusted that it would find its own targets?

But for what purpose? You did not simply go ahead and kill random people.

Was the purpose of the attacks to harm Madeleine and the reputation of her train line? Was there a madman among the four possible suspects who wanted nothing more than to wreak maximum havoc—just because he hated Madeleine?

That sounded no less crazy than the scenario with the trained killer spider, Penny had to admit to herself, because in that case anyone could have been killed. If the assassin wasn't careful, in the end even he could've fallen victim to it himself.

No, that was complete nonsense. She was going around in circles with her hair-raising theories.

She was particularly tormented by the confounded steak knife with which Madeleine had been killed. Assuming that the killer really had had the spider under his control, why on earth had he resorted to a new weapon in Madeleine's case? Why hadn't he simply put his killer creature to work a third time?

With the knife attack, the perpetrator had exposed himself. He had made a huge mistake. Before Madeleine's stabbing, no one had even suspected that Xavier or Jacques might have been the victims of a murderer. Why on earth would someone attract the attention of the criminal investigations department with such an obvious bloody act as a knife attack, if he had gotten away with the mysterious but unexplained spider bites? That was the big question. To which Penny knew no answer, no matter how hard she wracked her brain.

And finally, there was the question of motive, which remained equally puzzling. *Why* had Xavier and Jacques had to die, if they had indeed been the intended victims? What reason would Erika have, for example, to kill her husband's two brothers?

Well, the three men had not been friends, but that was hardly a sufficient reason to murder someone. Had Erika and her husband hatched a plot against Jacques and Xavier? With the help of trained spiders? Penny didn't believe either of them capable of such creativity. But she could be mistaken. Hatred probably fired the imagination just as much as great love.

And what about Louise? Had she wanted to get rid of her fiancé, whom she obviously loved so much? And also killed his brother, for some outlandish reason? Or, in the end, had Schneiders had something against the wayward offspring of her boss? Against those two who did not work in the company, as Martin did?

These theories were about as far-fetched as they could get, Penny told herself in frustration.

16

"Let's question the witnesses," Penny said to the doctor. Strange, she thought at the same moment, that the police still had not arrived.

On the other hand, even in the 21st century one was at the mercy of the forces of nature when they acted up as they were doing tonight. Presumably the officers Dr. Stiller had called were as stuck in their vehicles as any civilian motorist who had gotten lost in the raging snowstorm.

"The suspects, you mean to say?" the doctor replied grimly.

Penny nodded. People can be so different, she pondered. This man was not nearly as eager as she to solve this murder case into which they had both stumbled by accident. You could tell Dr. Stiller took his medical duties very seriously, but otherwise wanted to get off this train as quickly as possible.

Penny, on the other hand... what exactly did she want? She could not deny that she was frightened, but there was something else, too. Something that was much stronger than any fear. The desire to hunt, the insatiable urge to uncover what the heck had happened on this train, and the ambition to solve this case before she had to hand it over to the police.

There was certainly not much time left before the officers would finally arrive. And she absolutely wanted to talk to the four suspects first. At least briefly.

Maybe it was ridiculous to want to play the amateur sleuth in this murder case. It was a strange, no, a bizarre case, certainly a good three sizes too big for her. *But still*, she decided, *I'll give it a try. What have I got to lose?*

Your life, maybe? A warning voice spoke up in the back of her head. The murderer was among these four people. He knew how to hide himself well, but he had also proven that he was ruthless and would take any risk if someone got in his way. Madeleine had already paid for her suspicions with her life. Penny had to be careful that she did not suffer the same fate.

"Let's start with the assistant," she said to Dr. Stiller. "After that, we'll take on the family."

The doctor nodded wordlessly, and they got going together.

Christiane Schneiders had obeyed Penny's request to remain in her compartment. She seemed to have fully recovered from the shock she had suffered at the sight of her murdered boss. She was talking on her cell phone when Penny and Dr. Stiller entered the compartment. Her voice still sounded a little rough, but otherwise the assistant had probably adopted the motto *The Show Must Go On*.

The phone conversation seemed to be about a legal

dispute with some Chinese supplier to the Salmann group of companies.

"We really need to talk to you," Penny interjected when Schneiders stopped talking for a moment in order to listen to her interlocutor.

The assistant nodded her understanding, promised the Chinese guy she would call him back as soon as possible, and then switched off her cell. Her eyes looked tired, but still she looked at Penny expectantly.

"How can I help?" she asked dutifully. "Any new developments?"

"We just have a few questions for you," Penny replied. "I'm afraid there are no new findings so far. And the police haven't arrived yet, either."

Schneiders made a hand gesture toward the window panes, through which one could barely make out anything except a diffuse, swirling white. "It's a miracle if anyone will get through to us at all," she said.

Penny agreed with her, nodding. Then she began her questioning: "Do you have any idea if Madame Salmann's sons had made enemies? Personally... or even professionally?"

The assistant's eyes widened. Instead of answering Penny's question, she said, "So you think Madame was right in her suspicions, do you? That her sons were indeed murdered? But how in the world—"

"We can't know for sure yet, Ms. Schneiders," Penny interrupted her. "I'm just trying to gather some facts—which I will, of course, provide to the police."

Penny felt quite strange about striking such a matter-of-fact tone. But it was important that the super capable assistant take her seriously, see her as competent. That was the only way this conversation could yield any useful information.

Schneiders nodded. "Yes, of course. I see. The answer is no. I don't know of any enemies Jacques or Xavier could have made. Not within the family, anyway."

She looked at Penny intently. "That's what you're assuming, isn't it? That someone from the family did it? No one would have gotten through to Madame from the rear carriages in order to—" Schneiders hesitated, cleared her throat, and then said, making an effort to keep her voice firm, "To shut her up."

"You're right about that," Penny replied. "Forgive me for putting this so bluntly, but I got the impression that there was some animosity within the family. Wasn't there?"

Schneiders twisted her mouth into a pained smile.

"I suppose there's no denying that. Madame loved her sons, I know that, but she was often very... well, strict with them. And they disappointed her in many ways, too, I'm afraid."

Penny nodded. She had gotten that impression herself. But Madeleine was out of the question as her sons' murderer. She was dead herself now, and she certainly hadn't plunged the steak knife into her neck with her own hand.

"I just can't imagine anyone in the family being capable of such a heinous crime," the assistant continued. "Even if they don't like each other very much. I've known them all for a very long time—with the exception of Mademoiselle Louise. She and Monsieur Jacques got engaged only recently. But she's certainly not a murderer either, I'm sure of that."

Penny registered out of the corner of her eye how Dr. Stiller nodded vigorously at these words. He, too, apparently did not believe the beautiful young woman to be capable of murder.

Neither do I, Penny thought. But one of these four people, who all seem so harmless, had to be the killer. Or was she missing something?

At that moment, a memory stirred in the back of her mind. It was just a small thing she had noticed at dinner: the strange look Schneiders had given Erika Salmann. The prime suspect, as things stood at the moment.

Penny decided to ask the assistant about it. "What did you see that seemed so unusual?" she asked.

Schneiders hesitated for a moment. "Oh, surely it doesn't mean anything."

"You never know," Penny replied. "The more you tell me, the better." She gave the secretary a smile that she hoped was encouraging.

Schneiders relented. "Whatever you say. But it's really just a trifle. I just noticed that Madame Erika stowed a pill box in her purse."

"There doesn't seem to be anything unusual about that, in fact," Penny said—trying hard to hide her disappointment. "These days, everyone's taking pills, vitamins, et cetera."

Schneiders nodded. "It's just that Madame Erika never takes any medication. Orally, I mean. She has an inhibition to swallow or whatever it's called."

"You're really well informed," Penny said, and in the next moment was already thinking about what else might have been in the pillbox.

"As I said, I have been working for Madame Salmann for a very long time," Schneiders replied. "And as you can see, I'm often involved in private trips as well. So it has been inevitable for me to get to know her family very well, too."

"How big was this pillbox Erika stashed in her purse?" Penny asked.

"Maybe four by six centimeters," Schneiders estimated after thinking about it for a moment. The look she gave Penny seemed uncomprehending. But then her eyes suddenly widened. "You don't think that—" she began, but then abruptly broke off.

The assistant was really quick on the uptake. Of course, Penny was thinking exactly that: such a box might be the ideal container for the inconspicuous transport of a spider. The doctor had claimed that the critter in question had to be a smaller creature, judging by the size of the bite marks.

The assistant's head seemed to be spinning. Something was bothering her, a thought that Schneiders didn't voice but that seemed to trouble her deeply.

"What's wrong, Schneiders?" Penny asked, without hesitation. "You know that I only want to help. And that anything you share with me I will keep confidential."

The assistant nodded but said nothing. Penny gave her some time, and finally Schneiders leaned forward and spoke. "I'd just remembered that there was an incident once," she said hesitantly. "I don't know anything for sure; Madame Salmann only hinted at it."

"Yes?" Penny encouraged her.

"It was about a death... from spider venom. As far as I understand, it happened a long time ago."

"A death?" repeated Penny incredulously. "In Madeleine's circle of friends?"

Schneiders shook her head. "No. It did not concern my boss, but Madame Erika. But, as I said, I'm not familiar with the finer details."

A sudden silence spread in the compartment. It was as if the assistant had just dropped a bomb.

Erika Salmann had a history with spiders? Had been involved in an incident with a fatal outcome? That couldn't possibly be a coincidence! Penny's thoughts were racing.

Dr. Stiller seemed to be able to read from her face what was going through her mind. "Maybe we should talk to Erika next?" he suggested.

"Yes," Penny said. "We definitely should. "

17

When Penny and the doctor stepped out into the corridor, they were met by a figure that at first glance appeared to be a ghost. She wore a long flowing robe, had tangled hair and looked at them out of empty eyes.

At second glance, the robe was merely a floor-length nightgown and the ghost was Louise. She swayed slightly and leaned on the handrail of the aisle as though the train were still moving, as if it were just going through a curve at high speed. Had the young woman been drinking?

"Oh, it's you," Louise gasped as Penny stepped into her path. "Where is everybody? It's so quiet around here."

The doctor stepped forward, carefully grabbed her by the elbow and gently steered her along the corridor. "Come," he said, "we'll get you back to your compartment. You'll be more comfortable there."

"But I wanted to see Madeleine," Louise protested. "She certainly needs me. I must stand by her in this difficult hour—now that Jacques is no longer with us." She pronounced the name of her late fiancé like that of a saint.

Penny gave the doctor a questioning look. *Should we tell her? That Madeleine is dead?*

The doctor shook his head, barely perceptibly, and Penny couldn't blame him. The young woman was clearly in shock. After losing her fiancé, to also learn that Madeleine had been murdered would surely be too much for her. The truth, in all its horrible magnitude, could wait until the police arrived.

Dr. Stiller led the young woman through the airlock between the train cars and then back to her compartment. Penny followed right behind.

Without resistance, Louise allowed herself to be escorted to the sofa, where the doctor gently pressed her into the soft cushions. She lifted her head, and Penny could see that there were tears in the corners of her eyes.

"Xavier," she began in a toneless voice, "he was... not a nice person. But Jacques? An angel. How could this misfortune befall him? It's so unfair. "

Penny made no reply. Louise could also be informed at a later time that the two deaths of Jacques and Xavier had not been accidents, as they had all assumed in the beginning.

Nevertheless, Penny wanted to ask Louise at least a few innocuous questions. There might not be an opportunity for that later. "In what way was Xavier not a nice person?" she inquired, as gently as possible.

Louise looked at her uncomprehendingly—as if she first had to remember that she herself had made this claim only thirty seconds ago. But then she made a visible effort to regain her composure.

"Didn't you notice yourself?" she said. "His attitude toward women? He despised us—that's the truth. Even though he pretended to be a gentleman; it was mere sport to him. He saw women as conquests, nothing more. As game to be hunted. He didn't care about—"

She faltered briefly. Then she added, "He didn't care for... the women he slept with." She pressed her full, beautifully curved lips together until only a thin line was visible.

Penny couldn't help thinking that Louise had actually meant to say something else. "He didn't care for *me*." That was probably how the sentence should have ended originally.

What Louise had to say about Xavier largely coincided with Penny's own opinion of the dead man, but there was so much pain and contempt in Louise's words. It had to be something personal.

Had Jacques's beautiful fiancée made a closer acquaintance with Xavier? And if so, had her fiancé known about it? Was this perhaps the motive behind the murders? A love triangle? A drama of jealousy?

A thought occurred to Penny. What if Jacques had set the spider on Xavier, and then only by an unfortunate coincidence had himself become the second victim of his eight-legged ally? Because, in the presence of all the people gathered in Penny's compartment, he had failed to capture the spider inconspicuously or render it harmless?

It was possible. But then, who had killed Madeleine after Jacques was long dead? And why?

"What do you actually do for a living?" Penny asked, turning again to Louise, who was now wiping away her tears with the back of her hand. It couldn't hurt to learn a bit more about her—even if Penny hardly believed this woman, so amiable and now seemingly completely unhinged, to have been capable of committing one murder. Or even three.

Louise dug out a badly crumpled handkerchief from between the sofa cushions and blew her nose. "I'm a psychologist," she said—much to Penny's amazement. "I help ex-cons with job reintegration."

That didn't exactly sound like a profession where you could afford to be squeamish. And now this breakdown? How did that fit together?

Maybe she'd just loved her fiancé more than anything? And couldn't cope with his loss? Penny pondered.

After all, that was possible. Even a psychologist could suffer a severe shock in such a situation.

"So how did Jacques and you originally meet?" she continued her interrogation.

Something strange flashed in Louise's eyes. But the next moment it had already disappeared, and she said in a matter-of-fact tone, "I originally knew Xavier. He introduced me to his brother because we had some common interests. Climbing, trekking, paragliding. Xavier joked that I would be the ideal woman for Jacques... and he was so right about that. We knew straight away that we belonged together, from our very first meeting. Forever," she added, barely audible. She started to sob again.

"Listen, Miss Küfer," Dr. Stiller intervened, looking sternly at Penny. "Miss Louise needs rest now. We mustn't exert her any further."

"That's all right," Louise protested weakly, but Penny nodded at the doctor. They had to go on to Erika anyway, and then talk to Martin as well.

"What a lovely woman," the doctor said as he and Penny stood back outside in the corridor.

Penny agreed, but was still preoccupied in her mind with Louise's testimony. The words *psychologist, ex-con, climbing* and *paragliding* were haunting her.

"Sorry," the doctor added. "I guess it's pretty inappropriate to say something like that... about a suspect. Isn't it?"

Penny shrugged her shoulders. "Well, you're right. She is beautiful. One could turn green with envy. And I can't for the life of me imagine her as a ruthless murderess. She also has a very endearing manner, I must say. I think that's how she even won Madeleine's heart."

"Which was generally not very receptive to conquest," the doctor said.

Penny shot him an intrigued glance. "Did you know

her well, then? Madame Salmann?"

"Not all that well," Dr. Stiller replied. "I just treated her regularly during the winter months. She enjoyed spending time in St. Anton."

Penny moved towards the nearest window and peered into the snowy wasteland the train station had turned into.

We're locked in here, went through her mind. *Completely isolated. With a killer on the loose.*

She turned back to Dr. Stiller. "She seems so harmless, doesn't she? Louise, I mean. As though butter wouldn't melt in her mouth. And as if she were utterly helpless and lost now that her fiancé is dead."

The doctor nodded. "That's true. I can't deny that she, um, inspires a certain protective instinct in me."

"In me, too," Penny said. "But don't you think that's strange? She's not afraid of dangerous sports, has a degree in psychology, and works with ex-cons. She should be pretty hardened, shouldn't she? What if she's just putting on an act?"

"You don't think—" The doctor let the sentence hang unfinished in the air and shook his head violently.

"That she is our murderer? No, I can't imagine it, I've already said as much. But that's precisely why we shouldn't rule it out."

"I'm afraid I don't understand."

"Louise is a psychologist," she said. "Surely that means she's good at reading people. And manipulating them when necessary? Right? She's certainly capable of deliberately behaving in a way that makes us think she's an innocent, above suspicion. And if she's dealing with ex-cons, she may have learned a thing or two from them. "

"About *murder,* you mean?" the doctor asked, visibly indignant.

Penny nodded. "Also, someone who ventures into sports like paragliding is willing to take risks, which must be true of our killer. Stabbing Madame Salmann was a huge risk. The crime was committed in an extremely narrow window of time, and the killer couldn't rule out being observed by someone on his way to Madeleine's compartment—or on the way back after the murder."

"I see what you mean," the doctor said, still in a heated tone. "Nevertheless, I'm one hundred percent sure Louise is not our murderer!"

"Well, let's hope you are right, doctor."

18

Compared to Louise, Erika made a downright calm impression. She seemed to have regained her composure remarkably quickly after the night's events.

When Penny and Dr. Stiller entered her compartment, she was standing at the window staring up at the concrete wall that kept thousands of tons of rock from burying St. Anton's train station. Tonight, however, the snow seemed to want to compete with the rock. If it kept snowing like this, the whole train would end up disappearing under the mass of white.

Penny decided to get straight to the point. Perhaps she could draw Madeleine's daughter-in-law out with a very direct question.

"Do you know anything about spiders, Mrs. Salmann?" she began, looking quizzically at her interlocutor and eagerly waiting for her reaction.

Erika grimaced in disgust. "I hate spiders," she exclaimed, "I have a downright phobia of those vermin!"

She took a step toward Penny. "Why do you ask? Did you find the spider? You don't think *I* brought it on board, do you?"

When Penny didn't immediately give an answer, she added angrily, "You can't be serious? Why on earth would I want to murder my family?"

"You tell me," Penny replied. The strategy of provocation, of drawing Erika out, was coming along quite nicely.

Erika snorted. "Frankly, I don't care what you think. I don't have to talk to you, even if you think you can act like a policewoman and a judge at the same time."

"Your mother-in-law hired me to investigate the case just before she died. You know that, don't you? I'm just trying to help. I'm sure you're also interested in solving the murders, aren't you?"

"Of course! But if you want to see the murderess in *me*, you are only wasting your time."

Penny nodded, forced a smile, but then went on the offensive again. "Would you be so kind as to show me your pillbox, Mrs. Salmann?"

Erika looked at her uncomprehendingly. "I don't own anything like that. I can't swallow pills."

"I happened to see you stowing one of those little boxes in your purse at dinner," Penny replied.

It was a lie, obviously. Schneiders had made this observation, not Penny herself. But never mind. The end justified the means. Disclosing your witnesses was not a good idea; that much was common sense. You didn't have to be a trained detective to understand that.

"You are mistaken," Erika shot back in a cutting tone of voice.

Penny persisted. "Would you mind if I took a look in your purse?" she asked. This time she didn't even try to put on a smile. As far as hypocrisy went, she'd always been pretty darn bad.

"You bet I mind," Erika said. "I'm certainly not going to let you ransack my belongings! " She crossed her arms in front of her chest and stared Penny down.

"Ladies, please!" Dr. Stiller interjected. "We are working together here, aren't we?"

He didn't seem to have any trouble putting on a friendly smile, one that seemed authentic. But even as he spoke, he approached the desk on which a rather sizable handbag made of burgundy leather had been placed.

Without further ado, he grabbed the purse and dumped its contents on the desk.

Erika let out a cry that reminded Penny of a hissing cobra.

"How dare you!" she yelled at the doctor, but he displayed an agility and boldness that Penny would never have believed him capable of. With a few quick movements, he rummaged through Erika's belongings, and the next moment he was already triumphantly holding up the corpus delicti—a pillbox made of white plastic.

"That's not mine," Erika protested. "You planted that on me, admit it!" She stormed toward the doctor and tried to snatch the pill box from him.

He, however, quickly passed the small container to Penny.

Reflexively, she grabbed it. Great, she thought at the

same moment, we'll be leaving lots of misleading fingerprints on this piece of evidence. But at least she had caught Erika in a lie. And a pretty bold one at that.

But why all this fuss over a pillbox? Erika could have simply admitted she had one in her possession. That was still no proof that she had misused the small container to transport spiders. She could have simply claimed that her swallowing inhibition was a thing of the past, and that she had taken a headache tablet or something similar during dinner.

Penny took a closer look at the small white plastic box that the doctor had passed to her, while he was having a heated discussion with Erika. Thankfully, he was able to keep the now very angry woman in check.

A moment later, Penny realized why Erika had by no means wanted to reveal the pill box. The small plastic container was not only completely empty, it also had a tiny hole!

Penny spotted it in one of the corners of the box. The hole was so small that you had to look very closely not to miss it, and it looked as if someone had taken great pains to drill it neatly.

Air supply for the spider, was all Penny could think.

When she raised her voice and attracted the others' attention to the hole, they both fell silent. In the doctor's face she could read a clear echo of her own thoughts. The spider had been transported in this box!

And the box had been in Erika's handbag. Which she had not wanted to be searched at any price.

If this was not serious evidence! Progress at last!

But still, wasn't it incredibly stupid to keep such an incriminating piece of evidence with you? And Erika Salmann might be all kinds of things, but she was not a stupid person. The police would probably believe her if she claimed that the box had been planted on her. Was this her very strategy? Wasn't it the best proof of innocence to foist conspicuously incriminating evidence on oneself, which could easily have been gotten rid of? Had Erika kept the box—not because she was stupid, but out of this very intelligent calculation?

Penny's euphoria over the new piece of evidence died down in one fell swoop. Was the discovery of the pillbox not the breakthrough she had been hoping for, after all? Had she merely fallen into the very trap that a perfidious murderess—Erika—had set for her? Had she merely stumbled upon what she was supposed to find? Or was she overthinking things, and Erika was guilty in the end?

Penny groaned inwardly. Then she asked the doctor a direct question, heedless of Erika's presence. "What do you think, doctor, is this box big enough to house the kind of venomous spider we're probably dealing with? This funnel-web spider, or whatever it's called?"

The doctor nodded without hesitation. "I'm sure it is," he said.

19

"Your mother is dead. She was murdered," Penny told Martin Salmann. It was almost inhumane to make this announcement so directly and brutally, but she wanted to watch Martin's reaction.

The surprise and shock reflected in his eyes could not have been more convincing. If Martin had killed his mother, he was an extremely gifted actor.

But wasn't that exactly what distinguished psychopaths from regular folks? That they could disguise themselves perfectly and were often perceived by their environment as harmless average citizens or even bores? Sometimes for decades.

Martin had waited obediently in his suite as Penny had told him to, and he offered no resistance when she now asked him to answer a few questions for her. He seemed to be still busy digesting his mother's murder—followed by the horrible realization that his brothers' deaths must have been murder as well.

It was more bad news at once than a person normally had to deal with in their whole life. Three murdered family members in one night... Martin was holding up remarkably well for that. Fortunately, he didn't pester Penny with questions about the details, but just sat there paralyzed.

"Who could have had something against your two brothers?" she began her amateurish interrogation. "Do you know of any enemies?" Penny deliberately kept the question general, though it should have been: *enemies within the family.* Would Martin think of that on his own?

"Enemies?" he echoed. "Well, Xavier has certainly, um, antagonized one or the other husband, if you know what I mean. But other than that? I don't think so. And as for Jacques—"

His voice trailed off. He seemed distracted, as if his mind was occupied with a completely different question. A far more pressing one. He stared past Penny into nowhere, chewing on his lower lip. His brow furrowed deeply.

"Would you like to share your thoughts with us?" she prompted him.

Martin winced. "What? Oh, no, it's nothing." He lowered his gaze, looking down at his hands, which he held folded in his lap as if to say a prayer.

"Are you sure about that?" Penny probed. "You know how it is: every little detail, no matter how insignificant, can be decisive in the end. You do care about bringing the killer to justice, don't you? He has wiped out half your family."

"Yes, yes, you're right." Martin looked over at Dr. Stiller, who had taken a seat at the desk and was silently following the course of the conversation. Then he hunched his shoulders and groaned. "Oh, it will come out after all; at the latest with the police. Maybe you can advise me how to handle it. After all, it's probably just a stupid coincidence."

"Go ahead," Penny said simply.

Martin rose shakily from the sofa and began to pace the compartment, as if he could better collect his thoughts that way. Then he dropped heavily onto the edge of the bed and groaned again.

"So, it's about Erika, my wife. It was ages ago, but... well, her first husband—his name was Pierre; he... he died of a spider bite. It happened when they were vacationing in Tuscany. It was an accident, of course!" he quickly added. "Erika had nothing to do with it." But he did not sound quite convinced himself.

Just a stupid coincidence? Penny certainly didn't believe that. People didn't die of spider bites every day, certainly not in Central Europe.

"Who knows about this incident?" she asked Martin.

"No one," he replied after a brief pause. "I'm sure you can imagine that Erika wouldn't tell anyone. It was a very traumatic experience for her. To lose her husband at such a young age and in such a tragic way."

"Really no one?" inquired Penny. Martin had hesitated at first in his answer, then spoken with exaggerated fervor. She couldn't help feeling that he was lying.

Martin shook his head, but then quickly averted his gaze.

Yes, definitely. He was lying. But to what end?

"Not even your mother?" Penny probed further.

"No," he shot back. "Certainly not."

Penny was not convinced. Maybe Madeleine had known about Erika's past after all, even if Martin didn't want to admit it. Was that why she had suspected her daughter-in-law of murdering her sons?

Perhaps that was why the old lady had sent for Penny just before she had been killed herself—because she had wanted to tell her about that very incident from Erika's past. But she had been silenced by her daughter-in-law just in time.

Didn't Erika have to expect, though, that her past would come to light in the end? At the latest, when the police began their investigation? And wasn't it crazy—no, stupid in this case—to use a poisonous spider as a murder weapon?

Had Erika hoped that the two deaths on the train would again pass as accidents, just as with her ex-husband? And did that mean that she had also murdered him as well?

Penny felt like her head could burst at any moment.

Dr. Stiller's cell phone rang. He pulled it out of the pocket of his jacket and answered the call. He listened for a moment, then nodded vigorously and said. "Yes, right away." He then hung up.

"The police are here," he announced. "I'll see that the inspector is let in." The next instant he had already scurried out of the compartment, and Penny was left alone with Martin.

He looked up at her. "I suppose I should receive the police officer, shouldn't I? I am, after all, the head of the family now." The way he looked while making this suggestion showed he was dreading the mere thought of having to face the inspector.

Penny nodded. "You can do this. I'll stay by your side and tell the policeman what happened, if you like."

"Oh, yes, thank you," Martin said. He rose wearily from the edge of the bed and headed for the door.

Like a man on his way to execution, went through Penny's mind.

20

The policeman who had just climbed into the train at the rear end of the carriage was on his own. At first glance, he looked like a yeti.

At second glance, he was just a very tall, lanky young man who had wrapped himself up as if for a polar expedition. And he was covered with snow from head to toe.

He was getting rid of the snow now, unknotting his scarf, patting his jacket off, visibly embarrassed that he was leaving quite a mess on the Occident Express's spotless carpet in the process.

"Inspector Jürgen Moser," he introduced himself. "Sorry it took so long. We—oh, I'll spare you all the mishaps. Just about everything that could possibly go wrong went wrong!" he said with fervor. Then he took off his gloves and rubbed his hands together.

He first extended a half-frozen hand to Penny, then greeted Martin in the same way, while the doctor who had let him in was already receding into the background.

Penny eyed the young policeman. He could be in his early twenties at most, quite a bit younger than herself. "You're on your own?" she asked him. "No colleagues?"

Inspector Moser nodded. "Yes. As I said, total chaos tonight. We have two missing tourists, impassable roads, broken down trucks, serious accidents, even one of our service vehicles—"

He broke off and contorted his face in agony. "I had to make my way here mostly on foot. Traffic is completely blocked. On the entire Arlberg."

"And the Major Crimes team?" asked Penny.

The inspector frowned. "Don't expect them before noon today. At the moment we are completely cut off from the outside world. So you'll have to make do with me for now, I'm afraid."

He took off his thick, snow-encrusted winter jacket and let it fall to the ground. Underneath it, his police uniform was revealed, which could have used some ironing.

Martin took a step forward and cleared his throat.

"I am the son of Madeleine Salmann. The—" He faltered, swallowed hard. "Who was murdered tonight. Just like my two brothers." His voice sounded shaky, and the short sentences he had uttered came across as if he had rehearsed them two hundred times in his mind.

With a wave of his hand toward Penny, he stepped back again and let her take the stage. "Before she died, my mother hired this young detective who happened to be on board," he said. "Miss Penny Küfer. Mother asked her to investigate the case until you arrived,

Inspector. She can tell you everything that happened."

"Aspiring detective," Penny corrected him, mumbling sheepishly. She fervently hoped the young policeman wouldn't burst into laughter at this announcement. Or worse.

But Jürgen Moser took note of the information and just nodded his head as a matter of course.

Martin gave the policeman a docile look. "Excuse me, please," he said. With those words, he dashed away and disappeared into the compartment where Penny had temporarily placed him as part of her witness isolation operation. The suite, right next to her own, which Xavier had originally occupied.

You could hear the door to the bathroom being pushed open and slammed shut again. Then came muffled but unmistakable choking sounds. Martin, the new head of the Salmann family, was throwing up.

"Nerves," Dr. Stiller said apologetically. "It was a bit much for all of us tonight."

The young cop nodded and gave Penny a winning smile. "I can imagine," he said. His Tyrolean accent was strong, and his voice sounded warm and compassionate.

Penny had actually expected to be greeted in a rather hostile way by the official representative of the law. Most police officers weren't too fond of private detectives. They often looked down on them, considering the private eyes annoying competitors, amateur sleuths, or even charlatans who stuck their noses into things that were better left to the professionals.

Jürgen Moser, however, seemed to harbor no such prejudices. Penny breathed a sigh of relief. "Would you like some tea to warm up a bit?" she offered.

"Oh yes, that would be wonderful."

"I'll get one for you," Dr. Stiller said. "For both of you. And then I'm going to take care of Miss Louise for a bit, if you don't mind. The poor woman is very distressed."

"Of course." The inspector nodded.

"I'll show you the crime scene in the meantime, Mr. Moser," Penny offered. "Or rather, the crime scenes. Let's start with my compartment. Let me share everything I've been able to get my hands on so far. There are some leads I think you should follow."

She looked over her shoulder for the doctor, who had been present when she had been questioning the suspects. She had not yet had the opportunity to ask his opinion on the course of her amateurish investigation. But Dr. Stiller had already turned away and was walking rapidly toward the lounge car.

Penny led the inspector to her cabin. He was visibly surprised to find such luxurious suites on a train, but then dutifully turned his attention to the two dead bodies. Both Jacques and Xavier lay undisturbed where they had died. Xavier on Penny's bed, Jacques on the sofa.

Inspector Moser looked at the bodies only briefly and from a safe distance. "That's where the experts have to come in," he told Penny.

She got the impression that he had not yet seen too many murder victims in his career. As young as he was, he couldn't have been a member of the police force for too long.

As if he were able to read her thoughts, he asked her, "So you're a detective, Miss Küfer? Still in training, you mentioned earlier? How far along are you?"

Penny would have liked to sink into the ground. "Not very far yet," she said evasively. And quickly countered with a question of her own. "How long have you been on the force?"

She earned a shy smile. "I also just finished my training a few months ago," the inspector confessed. "And I've never yet had to deal with murder," he added after a brief pause. "But I would like to move in that direction later on. A career in criminal investigation, that's my greatest aspiration."

Again, he interrupted himself. "I don't know if I have what it takes, though."

Something lit up in the policeman's eyes that seemed like a reflection of Penny's own feelings and dreams: ambition, a desire to excel, coupled with curiosity and a great passion for solving mysteries.

"I'm sure you have what it takes," she said. The young inspector was very likeable, she had to admit to herself. So likeable, in fact, that it was easy to forget that he was a policeman and the official representative of the law at a murder scene.

Penny reflected. Was she flirting with this guy?

Dear me, you have a murder to solve! she chided herself. Three murders, to be exact.

She cleared her throat. And ventured an unusual advance.

"The snowstorm is our chance, Inspector," she said, "one that won't come around again any time soon. If we manage to solve this case before the Major Crimes team arrives—that would be fantastic for your career prospects, wouldn't it?"

"*We?*" the inspector asked. "Surely you are aware that I am not allowed to discuss a murder case with you? You're a civilian. No offense, Miss Küfer."

"Oh, please, do call me Penny. After all, we're practically the same age." She caught herself putting on her most charming smile, batting her eyelashes.

He hesitated for a moment, but then nodded. "Agreed." He shook her hand. "Jürgen. But that doesn't change the fact that I have to go by the rules, and must not discuss the case with you—"

Penny raised her hands in an appeasing manner. "Of course! I totally understand. But you are not discussing the case with me—I'm discussing it with you! Actually, we're just chatting about it. While we wait for the professionals. Or let's say you're taking my testimony. I tell you everything I have seen and heard. That would be well within the rules, wouldn't it?" More batting of the eyelashes.

Jürgen Moser chewed on his lower lip, which instantly made him look five years younger. Like a teenager feverishly considering whether it was worth doing something foolish.

Then he tilted his head and grinned.

"You're a real character, Penny! If you don't mind me saying so. But for all I care, let's chat a bit." He winked at her in turn.

His eyelashes weren't bad either, Penny noted. Thick and long—enviable. But now, enough of this flirting! *Get to work, Penny! This is your big chance!*

21

Before Jürgen Moser could change his mind, Penny began her briefing. Outside the compartment window the snow was still falling, as if it never wanted to stop. But in here it was comfortably warm.

She recounted the events of the night in as much detail as she could manage, describing to Jürgen the possible suspects, and emphasizing that the murderer had to be found in the front two carriages.

"No one could have come through from the back to murder Madeleine," she emphasized.

The inspector raised his eyebrows. "So, a murder within the family? Or else the assistant is guilty?"

"Right."

Next, Penny gave the inspector an overview of her amateurish interrogations. She was careful not to call them that. She spoke of *chats* she had had with her fellow passengers—just as she and Jürgen were merely chatting at that moment. Quite noncommittally, and totally within the framework of the law.

Well... almost. If you turned a blind eye. Or two.

She made an effort to reconstruct her "chats" with the suspects as verbatim as possible from memory. Which earned her an admiring look from the inspector.

You're really capable, his eyes seemed to say—and Penny had the feeling of spontaneously growing a few centimeters. The fact that the young inspector probably knew little more than herself when it came to a proper homicide investigation didn't bother her in the least.

"What's your take?" she asked him after a short pause. "Is it just a stupid coincidence, this business of Erika Salmann and the spiders?"

Strictly speaking, with this question she had definitely initiated a discussion of the murder case between a policeman and a civilian, but Jürgen Moser seemed far too absorbed in his thoughts to take offense.

She looked at him intently while he pondered the question. Yes, clearly, he loved puzzling over this murder case just as much as she did. He enjoyed playing the clever sleuth in a way that seemed no longer possible in today's world.

"I can't imagine that this is just a coincidence," he finally said. "On the other hand, the way you described this woman to me, she's by no means stupid. Would she really use the same murder method as with her first husband, *again*? And such an outlandish one at that? And afterwards keep the pillbox in her purse?" He shook his head in disbelief.

"That woman is most certainly not stupid," Penny said. "What if she's even pretty smart, and is intentionally making it look like someone is trying to frame her? That makes for a great proof of innocence, right? Plant enough evidence against yourself that everyone thinks you're being framed."

The inspector nodded hesitantly. "On the other hand, the fact that her mother-in-law wanted to talk to her about the two fatalities makes her seem guilty," he said. "It seems to me Madame Salmann suspected Erika of murder."

"Yes, but what if Madeleine really wanted to talk about Martin? Maybe she suspected him, the surviving brother, and wanted to confirm—or refute—her suspicions with her daughter-in-law?

"That's a possibility," Jürgen said. "Did you get the impression, then, that Madeleine had a close relationship with her daughter-in-law? "

"Not really. If you ask me, Madeleine had no close relationship with anyone. Except her husband. And he has been dead quite a while. He was murdered too, by the way. I just remembered. "

"What? How so?"

"Allegedly it was a robbery. He was shot in the middle of the street."

"Another coincidence?" the inspector said, more to himself than to Penny. "Or could the murders of the two brothers have been some kind of late revenge?"

"You think those two had something to do with their father's death?" That seemed pretty far-fetched to Penny. On the other hand, tonight's murders were just that. Bloody deeds within the family. So why not back then, too?

"Let's proceed methodically," Jürgen said, looking like a bloodhound on a hot trail. "We have a modus operandi—we know how the crimes were committed. One by steak knife, the others by spider. Although it seems strange to me that you guys didn't find the insect. I mean, it's got to be somewhere, right?"

Penny, who sometimes tended to be a bit of a know-it-all, was about to enlighten the inspector that spiders were not insects—as she herself had learned only tonight from Dr. Stiller. She managed to suppress the impulse to shine with this knowledge though, just in time, so as not to interrupt the nice chat the inspector was now so willingly holding with her by being a smart-ass. In the end, he would remember that he was very much bending his beloved rules.

"Surely the murderer could have just flushed the spider down some toilet," she said instead. "In fact, I'm sure he did—that's why he then had to silence Madeleine with the steak knife."

Jürgen Moser made an astonished face. "Yes, of course, that would be a possibility. Why didn't I think of that myself? The colleagues from Major Crimes will certainly be able to examine the train's sewage tanks. It should be possible to find the insect there."

Penny nodded. "They're closed systems these days, I suppose? Nothing just spills on the tracks like it used to."

She hesitated. "It's just, it doesn't really make sense...

The murderer would have been all right even if the spider had been found. Before Madeleine's murder, we all assumed the two deaths were an accident. A nasty and very strange accident, to be sure, but certainly not cold-blooded murder. And I also can't picture how the murderer got the steak knife. Or rather, when. I've been grappling with that question for hours, and I just can't find an explanation. I mean, he could have taken the flipping thing from the restaurant during dinner, or shortly afterwards at the latest—he just had no opportunity to sneak back into the restaurant *after* he learned that Madeleine suspected murder. In that case he would inevitably have been seen."

"It really doesn't make sense," the inspector said, scratching his head. He looked around the room, then his gaze shifted and lingered on the window pane. He stared out into the almost opaque whiteness and seemed to be thinking hard. He looked tired, but still very focused. Almost zealous.

Penny herself also felt quite exhausted. The night was almost over, but sleep was still out of the question. There would be time for that later, when they had hunted down the murderer. After all, the inspector wore a gun on his belt, which gave Penny a sense of security. She may have been locked in with a triple murderer, but now she was no longer at his mercy. Jürgen Moser might be young and inexperienced, but he would still make use of his weapon in an emergency. And he would be able to hit his mark—Penny had no doubt about that.

The inspector turned around, looked at her, and said, "Isn't it possible that someone killed the brothers with spider venom? But without a spider? Possibly, the critter wasn't found because the killer *injected* his victims with the poison? With a special device that caused the characteristic two holes? Maybe he only faked the bite of a spider?"

Penny shook her head.

"I told you no one was near the victim. At least in the first case. Xavier and I were, um, alone here in my compartment. Surely I would have noticed if someone had snuck in?"

Was there mistrust in the inspector's eyes? Surely he did not suspect her?

"Maybe you were, um, so busy that you both weren't paying attention to what was going on around you?" he said, looking a tiny bit embarrassed at those words.

"No," Penny said quickly. "We weren't... Well, I mean, we were still sitting around talking. In reasonably good lighting. There was definitely no one sneaking up on Xavier. Impossible!"

"No need to justify yourself, Penny," the inspector said. A meaningful smile flitted across his face. "Just because you wanted to have sex with a stranger."

"I'm not justifying myself at all!" she shot back. It was really nobody's business if she wanted to indulge in an erotic adventure. She was an adult woman, newly single, and could do as she pleased.

Why, then, was she so eager not to make a bad impression on this copper?

You like him, Penny; why not admit it to yourself?

22

Quickly, Penny pushed the thought aside and picked up the conversation again.

"No," she reiterated. "No human being killed those two men. Neither Xavier, nor Jacques, although in his case the room was full of people. Someone would have had to bend down and inject something into his foot. That would have been noticed. Not a chance."

"Then it must have been a trained spider after all," Jürgen Moser said. "It's not impossible. Just think of the Sherlock Holmes story with the trained snake. What was it called? *The Speckled Band*?"

"Yes. That's one of my favorites!" Penny replied excitedly. She had loved the Sherlock Holmes stories since she was a child. The eccentric—nowadays you would say nerdy—detective was one of her greatest heroes and role models.

"But you must know about all the criticisms of the story, right?" she said to Jürgen. "*The Speckled Band* is one of the most famous Sherlock stories, but also the one where Sir Arthur Conan Doyle did the sloppiest research."

"Seriously?" the inspector replied. The eager smile that had just spread across his face vanished.

That's great, Penny, you had to be a smart-ass after all! But now it was too late to back out. Now the ambitious young policeman was looking at her expectantly.

"Well, I only read it somewhere once," she retreated at least halfway. "It's like this: the murderer in the *Speckled Band* put a snake in the strongbox of his room, didn't he?"

Jürgen Moser nodded.

"And he trained this snake to crawl through a vent into the next room, where his victim was sleeping. There, the reptile slithers down a bell pull and kills the woman with its venom."

"Exactly. And after that, the killer calls the animal back to his room with a whistle, having trained the snake beforehand to this particular sound."

"Again via the bell pull and vent," Penny added. "And then he rewards the snake with a little bowl of milk."

"So where's the sloppy research?" asked Jürgen Moser.

"All over the place. First, you can't keep a snake in a strongbox—it would suffocate in there. But that's still the smallest problem. Second, a snake cannot climb up a loosely hanging rope like a bell pull. Third, snakes are deaf, so they can't hear a whistle. And fourth, they are lactose intolerant. So feeding them milk doesn't work either."

The inspector gasped. "Really?" he muttered, visibly shocked. Surely Conan Doyle, with his Sherlock Holmes stories, was also one of Jürgen Moser's heroes.

And Penny had just pretty much dismantled him.

But the young policeman quickly regained his composure. "Nonetheless," he said. "The spider could have been trained. By other methods. We can't rule that out."

At that instant, the melodious chime of the doorbell sounded. "Come in," Penny called out reflexively.

The door opened, seemingly as if by magic—for there was no one to be seen outside in the corridor. But then the little robo-steward rolled in, equipped with a tray on which he balanced two steaming teacups. And a small silver bowl with cookies.

"Wow," the inspector gasped. He had not yet made his acquaintance with the high-tech gadgets aboard the train. "What a cool little fellow."

The robo-steward drove toward him, stopped just in time—and Jürgen reached for one of the tea cups. The mechanical waiter then turned ninety degrees around its own axis, whirred on its roller feet towards Penny and stopped again.

When she had also taken her tea cup—plus the cookie bowl—the robot let out a sonorous "Thank you for your order," and left the compartment without further delay.

In that instant, an idea struck Penny. The thought literally exploded in her head at the very moment she burned her tongue with her first sip of tea.

"He can spot us!" she exclaimed, jumping up so abruptly that she almost spilled her tea.

"Huh?" the inspector asked. Hungrily, he eyed the bowl of cookies Penny had set down beside them on the desk. The poor man must not have eaten for countless hours because of all the emergencies tonight.

Penny handed him the cookies. "The robot!" she then said. "He knows where in the room we happen to be. He turned his face toward us. Well, his front, I mean."

The inspector shrugged his shoulders. "I'm sure he has plenty of sensors, and he moves autonomously. Like a self-driving car. Otherwise, he would bump into everything—or some staff member would have to control him remotely, which would make no sense. After all, these gadgets are supposed to save on personnel."

"And with these sensors, he can also tell where in a room we happen to be?" asked Penny. "But how can he tell us apart? How does he know who is a person and what's a piece of furniture or a wall? After all, he was coming right at us."

Jürgen shrugged his shoulders. "I'm not an expert in robotics. But I think he has cameras with which he can make out human contours. Microphones that locate our voices, and possibly even infrared, in which case he can also sense our body heat. Maybe every passenger who boards the train will be photographed, and the AI will know who's who for the whole journey. All feasible these days."

"The AI?" inquired Penny.

"Artificial Intelligence."

"Oh," said Penny. Futuristic technology wasn't her strong suit.

"The blessings of the 21st century," Jürgen said with a smile. "But what are you actually getting at?"

Penny didn't answer right away. She was still busy processing the new information with which the policeman had just bombarded her. She took a few sips of tea, more carefully this time so as not to burn herself again, while her brain worked at full speed.

Then she said, "You were wondering before if the spider venom wasn't administered in some other way. That is, without a spider. "

"Yes?"

"Don't you see? A human couldn't have done it—but possibly a robot could have! You might be able to train a spider somehow with difficulty, but I refuse to believe you can make it attack a specific person on command."

"But you can program a robot accordingly," the inspector said. He now seemed to understand what Penny was getting at.

"If I understood you correctly just now, that should be possible, right?" she asked excitedly. "To program an AI, as you call it, so that it moves on its own through the train and targets a certain person whose appearance you have stored in its memory beforehand. And make it attack this person. Inject them with poison."

"If the robot is equipped with the proper injection device, it shouldn't be a problem," Jürgen said. "And, of course, with a tank for the poison."

"He'd have to be much smaller than the robo-stewards, though," Penny pointed out. "Otherwise, we would have seen him. Even though those little gadgets are nowhere near as conspicuous as a human."

They looked at each other wordlessly for a few moments. "Very much smaller," she emphasised.

"That's feasible, too," Jürgen Moser said. "I like to read technology mags about such high-tech gadgets, you know. It's a hobby of mine. And just the other day I came across an article—about the potential applications of nanotechnology in medicine."

"Nano?" Penny interrupted him. "What's that, now?"

The inspector seemed to be completely in his element. Apparently, he was not only a passionate fan of criminology, but also quite a nerd.

"*Nános* means dwarf," he explained to Penny. "A nanometer is a billionth of a meter. Invisible to the naked eye. A human hair is about sixty thousand nanometers in diameter. And there are now robots on that tiny scale."

"For real?"

"Yes. Sounds incredible, doesn't it? The article I just mentioned, for example, was about medical nano-robots that can be targeted at cancer cells in the human body in order to destroy them. It's still in the experimental stage, but our hypothetical killer robot could be quite a bit bigger, after all, and would still be virtually invisible."

"That must be it! "Penny exclaimed, even though she understood only about half of what Jürgen was saying. "This is how the two brothers were murdered; with the help of one of those midget thingies! Madeleine Salmann ran the ultimate high-tech corporation. They produce all kinds of gadgets, drones, weapons, those cute robots you see here on the train and so on—why not something in the nano range?"

Jürgen nodded eagerly. "Why not, indeed. In the arms industry, you can already find plenty of micro- and nanotechnology, too."

"But surely not tiny little mechanical killer spiders?" said Penny. "Right?"

"Probably not. But someone with the relevant technical know-how could have adapted one of Salmann's products accordingly. For his own murderous purposes."

Penny fell silent.

"What's up?" asked Jürgen. "I think you're exactly on the right track with this idea. Our poisoner was a robot, not a spider! We started from a completely wrong premise."

"But no one on board this train has the expertise to create such a robot," Penny objected. "Or even to re-program an existing one. Well, except for Madame Salmann, of course. She was a technical genius. But she can't be our murderer. She was killed herself, after all. Although... What if she built one of those mini killer robots to poison her sons with? And then another family member took revenge on her?"

"It's possible," the inspector said. "Although I must admit that sounds rather lurid. A mother murdering her own children?"

"She considered them deadbeats," Penny said. "But I admit that's hardly enough of a reason to kill them."

"If she did kill them," Jürgen replied thoughtfully, "perhaps she herself was then murdered by this Louise? She loved her fiancé very much, you said, didn't you? And now she's completely in shock. She could have taken revenge on the old lady—in the heat of the moment, with the steak knife."

"This really sounds like a dime novel," Penny objected.

"But it could be possible," the inspector insisted.

23

"We need to talk to the witnesses again," Penny said. "Or rather, to the suspects. You and me together!" She could barely contain her excitement.

Finally, they had made a breakthrough, taken a big step forward. A killer robot instead of a spider opened up completely new possibilities!

Jürgen Moser, who had just taken another look at the bite wounds of Xavier and Jacques, jerked upright.

"That's out of the question!" he protested. "If one of these people later tells the CID team that I interrogated them in your presence, I'll be out of a job."

Oh well. He wasn't wrong about that. In the fervor of her new insight, Penny had completely forgotten about that pesky detail.

You're not the official investigator on this murder case, she had to remind herself. As much as she loved that role.

They looked at each other in silence for a while. A feeling of embarrassment spread between them.

"I've got it," Penny suddenly exclaimed. "Why don't you talk to the passengers in the back two cars for once? You could inform them that we're going to be stuck here for a while, but that they have nothing to worry about. And you make sure everyone stays in their compartments, and that the outside doors are securely locked, too, so no one can escape."

"Are you going to tell me how to do my job now, too?"

"Not at all," Penny said quickly, putting on her most docile smile. "I just figured that in the meantime... well, I could go, completely unauthorized and behind your back, without you knowing anything about it..."

"Get to the point, Penny," the inspector interrupted her. He looked serious, but wasn't there the tiniest hint of mischievousness in his eyes?

"I could talk to the suspects again," she said. "Alone, behind your back, so to speak. Then you're off the hook as far as your rules and regulations are concerned. I mean, you can't be everywhere, after all, and if you happen to be securing the rear of the train, whereas I disobey your explicit orders to stay in my compartment like everyone else... *you* certainly can't be blamed for that!"

"You're really incredible, Penny," Jürgen said, shaking his head.

She wanted to see him smile and that he would go along with her crazy plan.

He, however, eyed her insistently, almost soberly. "You're not even a private detective yet. You have no professional license, no completed training—"

"I know that," Penny interrupted him. "But I really need to clarify a few points. And our suspects will talk to me. They've already accepted me as a private investigator—hired by Madeleine, the head of the family. That carries weight, even if the old lady is dead now. And none of them will have a problem afterwards with the fact that I, civilian to civilian, so to speak, chatted with them about the case. They *want* to talk. Three of them are innocent, and they're scared. They want to understand what happened on this train tonight."

"I'm not comfortable with that idea," Jürgen Moser said, but he sounded far less averse now.

"There is no risk for you," Penny insisted. "And none for me either. As I said, I'm just chatting among civilians."

"And what if the killer feels cornered by you, during your interrogation? Pardon me, during your civilian chit-chat? Have you thought about that? If I'm in the rear cars of the train so you can do your thing behind my back, how am I supposed to help you when you're putting yourself in danger?"

Without Penny being able to do anything about it, a warm feeling spread inside her. Jürgen Moser was doing an excellent job in the role of protector. She liked that he cared about her.

That's just his cop instinct, she admonished herself. *You don't have to conclude that he likes you.*

"I can take care of myself," she told him. But secretly she had to admit to herself that he was right to object. Her plan could be dangerous. And she wasn't half as fearless as she pretended to be.

"The murderer could hardly have obtained another weapon, could he?" she said, although she was by no means certain of this fact. They were obviously dealing with a very creative person, one who was determined to do anything. After three murders, a fourth certainly didn't make a big difference.

Jürgen Moser sighed. He seemed to be thinking back and forth about whether he should agree to Penny's crazy plan.

"Let me try," she urged him. "If I can find something out, then you've solved the case. Deal? I don't need credit; I just want to help."

"Do you think I care about the laurels?" Jürgen replied sharply.

"But you want to solve the case just as much as I do! Don't you? And you could take the murderer into custody until your colleagues from Major Crimes finally arrive. Then he can't do any more harm, and the people on the train would be safe again. Wouldn't that be something?"

"Heck! For all I care, go ahead!" Jürgen contorted his face into a grimace that looked half like resignation, half like anger. And there was a hint of amusement, too.

Then he turned away and got ready to leave the compartment. In the doorway, however, he turned around again.

"Be careful, for heaven's sake, will you? If you even

get a bad feeling, get out at once—you have to promise me that! Wait, I'll give you my cell phone number. Keep your phone handy, and at the first sign of danger..."

"I'll call you right away!" Penny completed his sentence. "Yes, I will. I promise!"

They exchanged phone numbers, then the inspector disappeared into the corridor. He left the compartment door open behind him and moved away in the direction of the lounge car.

Penny, on the other hand, sought out Louise's compartment—not to question Jacques's fiancée again, but to discuss an important point with Dr. Stiller. In Penny's estimation, no promising trail of evidence led to Louise. Although one was not supposed to jump to conclusions.

The doctor raised his head as Penny entered the compartment. He was sitting next to Louise on the sofa. She was slumped over. It appeared as if she had fallen asleep.

It suited Penny just fine. With a jerk of her head, she motioned for the doctor to join her out in the corridor for a moment.

"I need to ask you something, Dr. Stiller," she whispered to him.

He immediately complied with her request. Almost silently, he stood up, crossed the suite and carefully closed the compartment door behind him, as gently as a father who did not want to wake his sleeping child.

Then he looked at her with tired eyes.

"What's up?" he asked. "Anything new?"

"Possibly," Penny said evasively. "Here's the thing: if we assume a deadly spider venom—what quantity is actually required to murder a human being?"

The doctor looked at her uncomprehendingly. "Well, apparently the animal managed to kill two people in quick succession. Unusual, if that's what your question is about. But by no means impossible."

Penny shook her head. "That's not what I mean. What I want to know: what's the amount of poison needed to kill someone? Are we talking a few drops? Half a teaspoon? How much space would the poison take up? That's what I'm concerned with."

The doctor still looked confused. Nevertheless, he answered the question readily. "I'm not an expert, of course. But with such a highly toxic substance, a tiny amount is enough. After all, the animals are sometimes very small—I told you that already."

"Yes, two to three centimeters in diameter—for the spider," Penny repeated the view the doctor had expressed a few hours ago.

He nodded. "The amount of venom such an animal secretes when it bites is perhaps the size of a grain of rice in terms of volume, I would guess. Possibly even smaller. As I said, I'm not an expert. But I don't understand what you're getting at, Miss Küfer?"

"A grain of rice? Such a tiny amount?"

"Yes. Maybe even less. A few drops in principle. But

now please tell me—"

"I'll explain later," Penny interrupted him. "First I have to make a few more calls. In the meantime, will you stay with Louise?"

"Yes, sure," the doctor said. "I think she's stable now, but it certainly can't hurt to have someone around."

24

Erika Salmann had not moved from where she sat alone in her compartment, right at the spot where Penny had left her, and seemed deeply lost in thought.

"You again?" she said as Penny came up to her. "When are the police coming? When can we get off this train? I want to get out of here. Surely it should be possible to get a hotel in St. Anton by—"

"You'll have to be patient," Penny interrupted her. "The criminal investigators are on their way, but the roads are impassable at the moment. In the meantime, though, I have one more question for you."

Erika looked at her disinterestedly, while Penny feverishly thought about how best to conduct the interrogation she was planning. Because now it was no longer just a matter of chatting aimlessly, but of getting down to the nitty-gritty; about finding out the truth.

She had to get Erika Salmann to come clean. She had to find out whether this woman was the murderer. And if so, she had to be on her guard—every second she spent in this compartment, any little carelessness, could cost her her life.

Inconspicuously she squinted at the ground, but there was nothing there. No tiny robot armed with the venom of a deadly spider. At least not one that could be seen with the naked eye. Which might not mean anything, as Penny knew by now.

If the amount of poison sufficient to send a human being to the afterlife was as tiny as Dr. Stiller had described, the robot could be smaller than an ant. That was not in the nano-range that Jürgen had so enthusiastically introduced her to, but it was scary enough.

It was now completely clear to her why no one had seen anything when Xavier and Jacques had been murdered; not even the two victims themselves. The tiny robot could have followed her and Xavier into the compartment, where it had waited for the appropriate command from the killer. Then it had crawled onto Xavier's foot and stabbed. Perhaps twice in quick succession and close together to simulate the characteristic double holes of a spider bite.

In the next moment, it could have disappeared again. No one would have noticed such an attack, even in Jacques's case, although the compartment had been full of potential witnesses at the time of his death.

Penny turned her attention to Erika. She tried to recall everything she knew about interrogation techniques, which was deplorably little. Of course, in the mystery novels she liked to read, witnesses or suspects were questioned all the time, but the real professionals probably didn't go about it the way they did in those books.

On her reading pile at home was a textbook by an ex-FBI agent and another one by an Oxford professor. Both men had written thick tomes on how to get people to tell the truth—how to expose lies.

Penny had bought a lot of similar works lately. Everything imaginable that a good detective needed to know. If you wanted to become a top professional in your field, it wasn't enough just to complete the standard training.

Unfortunately, she had only read the blurbs of the two volumes so far. Despite all her good intentions for her professional future—now, when it really mattered—she had to rely on know-how from crime novels. And on her instincts. That had to be enough.

"You didn't tell me the truth earlier," she said curtly to Erika Salmann.

Erika raised an eyebrow, but still seemed uninvolved. As if she were only listening with one ear to a conversation that clearly did not interest her.

Penny wasn't fazed by that. "You have relevant prior experience with venomous spiders," she told her suspect outright. "I was told about the circumstances of your first husband's death."

This achieved the desired effect. Erika let out an angry hiss. She jumped up from the chair where she had been sitting in a slumped posture and snapped at Penny: "Who told you that? Martin, right? That bastard. He's trying to frame me. Get rid of me. But he won't get away with it, I tell you!"

"Get rid of you?" repeated Penny, who could hardly believe how violently Erika had reacted to her accusation.

The stout little woman stared at her gloomily. Her cheeks had reddened. Something had awakened in her eyes. *Hate*, Penny told herself. Clearly.

Erika took a step toward her, but Penny forced herself not to back away.

You mustn't show any fear, she admonished herself. That was unprofessional for the great private investigator she was trying to be, and possibly fatal if Erika was a murderer. To show such people that you feared them, to make them feel they had power over you, could provoke an attack.

Erika wrinkled the corners of her mouth contemptuously. "My marriage is a farce; I make no secret of that. It has been for a long time. Martin is only still with me because he can't afford a divorce."

"What about you? Why don't you leave him?"

Penny received no answer.

The hatred in Erika's eyes flared up again: "He has a mistress, that pig," she said. Her voice was rough and toneless. "For quite some time now. And now I think he wants to take the opportunity to get rid of me in a cost-effective way. By framing me for these murders."

She stepped even closer to Penny and stared her straight in the face. "Maybe you'd better ask *him* your questions, Ms. Private Investigator. I'm the wrong one. I didn't kill anyone."

"Both of your brothers-in-law died from spider venom, just like your first husband. That doesn't strike you as odd?" countered Penny. "The police will certainly find it interesting, I would imagine. You must admit that it can hardly be a coincidence."

"I don't care what you can or cannot imagine," Erika hissed. At that, she turned around and headed for the desk under the window.

Apparently exhausted, she slumped back into the chair. "You don't have anything on me at all, Miss Küfer, and if Martin thinks he absolutely has to regale you with this age-old story about my first husband, perhaps you should ask yourself what prompted him to do so. What purpose is he pursuing with it? Maybe *he* is your murderer."

"Would you believe him capable of killing his own brothers?" Penny replied. "What would he have to gain by such an act?"

"I don't know, a larger inheritance if his mother ever dies? That is, she did die, but of course no one could have expected that."

Something stirred in the back of Penny's mind, but she couldn't get a grip on the thought because Erika was already talking on, now highly agitated. "Madeleine was going to retire soon, you know. And sell off the company because she didn't see a worthy successor in any of her sons."

"Martin is the only one of the three who's employed at the company, isn't he?" asked Penny.

Erika nodded. "But he's a nobody there, let's not kid ourselves. Madeleine put him in charge of an insignificant team where he could do no harm. Those were her own words—and she reminded Martin of her opinion at every opportunity, believe me." She shook her head. "It's a terrible family."

She fell silent and seemed to be thinking about something. Penny had the feeling that she certainly wanted to talk now. And that her hostility had diminished somewhat.

"Jacques and Xavier were in favor of selling the business, you know," Erika continued. "Martin, on the other hand, wanted to get his mother to pass the company on to him. He would then have paid off his brothers. The necessary funds were available in the company's coffers. The Salmann group is very strong financially. Everything Madeleine touched literally turned to gold."

"What about you? Do you support your husband's endeavor?"

"I am, of course, in favor of Martin continuing to run the company. It's madness to simply sell off such a global company. It should remain in the family!"

Penny suspected that Erika must have actively supported her husband in his desire to take over the business—if she hadn't been the one who had given him the idea in the first place. Erika was an ambitious woman; there was no question about that.

But was she also a murderer? Had she killed Martin's brothers because they had spoken out in favor of selling the company? Was that finally the motive Penny had been looking for all night? Eliminating the mother-in-law in addition to the two brothers fit well into that concept. Especially if Madeleine had seen something, or suspected Erika to be the murderer because of her history with poisonous spiders.

"The enterprise value is over a billion euros, I assume?" asked Penny.

"You can add another zero to that," Erika replied snootily. "As I said, Madeleine knew how to turn every idea she had, every patent she filed, into gold."

"I guess your mother-in-law was a technical genius, wasn't she?" interjected Penny.

"Yeah, sure."

While Erika didn't seem to have loved her mother-in-law very much, she apparently did appreciate Madeleine's accomplishments as a businesswoman, and as an inventor.

"Have you yourself ever taken a closer look at the company's products, Mrs. Salmann?" continued Penny.

"Me? No. I've never been involved in the business."

"But you have some interest in the subject matter? For example, how good is your knowledge of robotics?"

Erika narrowed her eyes and stared suspiciously at

Penny. Could she have guessed what this question was about? Or rather, did she know exactly, because it was she who had abused one of the company's mini robots as a lethal weapon?

Instead of answering Penny's question, Erika shifted back to complaining about her husband.

"That mistress of Martin's, she works at the company too," she said, looking at Penny as if she would like to wring her neck.

Penny wanted to make a reply, but Erika didn't give her a chance to speak. The subject seemed to really excite her. "He's been cheating on me for years, the bastard! And he actually thinks I don't know about it! Maybe it's even someone on his team, who knows? He wouldn't be the first guy to bed his secretary."

She laughed harshly, baring her teeth. "The floozy must have terrible taste to find him attractive!"

"Did he confess to you that he has a mistress? Or how would you know?" asked Penny.

Martin's extramarital adventures didn't seem very relevant to the murder investigation, but she had to follow every possible lead. Maybe it was true that Martin wanted to frame his wife for the murders, if he himself had committed them. If she were convicted, Martin would go unpunished, *and* he could then devote himself entirely to his mistress, without having to go through an expensive divorce. Erika would disappear behind bars for many years. Two birds with one stone, so to speak.

It was true that Martin didn't exactly pass for a hunk, but compared to his sharp-tongued wife, he could certainly do a little better with a new girlfriend.

Maybe I'm finally getting a little closer to the truth, Penny told herself hopefully. Had Martin Salmann eliminated his brothers because they wanted to sell the family business? And had he adapted one of the company's mini robots so that it could simulate the bite of a poisonous spider, in order to frame his un-loved wife, in whose immediate environment a man had already died from a spider bite?

That wasn't a bad theory, Penny thought. At least the best one she had so far.

"Of course, Martin hasn't confessed a word to me about his affair," Erika pulled her out of her thoughts. "He's too much of a coward for that. But he doesn't have to," she added. "That's the kind of thing you no-tice as a woman, if you're not completely insensitive."

She looked challengingly at Penny. Which probably meant: *You* wouldn't notice anything like that.

Penny gave no reply.

"The usual warning signs," Erika said, waving her hand dismissively. "Women's perfume on his clothes, condoms in his wallet, working long hours in the eve-nings at the company—although, as I said, he's not a major player there. Not the kind of manager who's so indispensable that he has to work overtime day and night."

"And you assume this woman also works at the company?"

"Yes. I had that checked out. I hired someone in your line of work, my dear Miss Küfer. A private detective who has been monitoring my husband for several months. Martin does indeed spend long hours at the office, when no one in his department is working anymore. During those evenings I'm sure he's having sex with his mistress. When he comes home afterwards, he often has that typical smell of sex on him. He doesn't have a shower in the office, you know. And I have an exceedingly fine nose." As if for emphasis, she wrinkled her fleshy olfactory organ, and looked completely disgusted at the same time.

25

"This is ridiculous!" Martin Salmann exclaimed. "Erika suffers from paranoia. I don't have a mistress!"

Penny had gone into his compartment right after she had finished talking to his wife. He had seemed glad to see her, had even thanked her again for taking over the negotiations with the police, as he put it.

Now, however, there was a certain hostility in his eyes, even though it might have been directed at Erika, not Penny. If one asked unpleasant questions, one could probably expect nothing else.

"So you just work a lot, then, and that's why you spend so much time in the office so late at night?" inquired Penny.

"I'm certainly under no obligation to give you an account of my working hours," Martin retorted. "And I also don't see what relevance my private life should have to—" He faltered, glanced around as if he detested nothing more than this train compartment, then added with a jittery gesture of his hand, "To all of this. This disaster."

He looked very tired, and his nerves had long since frayed. His gratitude to Penny and the friendliness that went with it seemed to have completely evaporated by now.

But Penny was not deterred. "Do you actually produce miniature robots in your company?" she asked him, although she had long since been sure of the answer.

She watched Martin's reaction attentively, but was disappointed. Either he had himself very well under control, or the question actually seemed completely harmless to him. Irrelevant.

"Mini robots?" he repeated, in an almost bored tone of voice. At least he seemed glad that Penny wasn't pestering him about his love life.

"Yes, exactly. Tiny drones, nano-machines for military purposes or something like that."

Martin now looked downright confused. "Yes, of course. Micro and nanotechnology are among our most lucrative business fields, as far as I know. And so is the weapons business."

"As far as you know?"

He shrugged his shoulders. "Mother has built a global corporation. A huge conglomerate of companies, subsidiaries and product lines, in both the civilian and military sectors. Hardly anyone but herself has a real overview of everything, if you ask me. And I'm the manager of customer service in one of our civilian divisions. In the vehicle sector, if you want to know. I'm not that knowledgeable about weapons systems development and production. But why are you interested in this at all?"

Penny gave him no answer.

What now? she asked herself. Should she adopt a confrontational course? Martin seemed like a man who could be intimidated quite easily. He didn't like being cross-examined, but that was probably true of most people. Otherwise, however, Penny didn't rate him as hot-tempered, nor overly aggressive. Except for the fact that he was possibly a murderer.

If you want to get ahead, you have to be willing to take some risks, she decided. She took a step closer to him, but at the same time made sure she stayed near the door. Within reach of her escape route.

She looked Martin firmly in the eye. "Do you know what I think, Mr. Salmann?" she began, adopting a deliberately provocative tone. "You know your way around your company much better than you admit. You got yourself an ingenious weapon, a mini robot that you adapted to fake the bite of a poisonous spider, and you used it to kill your two brothers. Maybe you hated Jacques and Xavier for a long time—maybe you blamed them for your father's death, I don't know. Or maybe you were jealous because Jacques was able to talk your mother out of her money and Xavier could live off his female acquaintances while you had to work hard for your salary. And in a less than prestigious capacity, from what it sounds like to me. Besides, your brothers' passing also makes you the sole heir now that your mother is dead."

When she leveled this last accusation at Martin Salmann, something unexpected happened.

Afterwards, when everything was over, Penny had to admit to herself that her knowledge of human nature was not exactly proficient. But also, at the very moment Martin Salmann came at her, she had something like a vision. A sudden and radical realization that she had been looking at this murder case the wrong way around from the very beginning. And that was why she had run into a wall.

Martin's attack came only fractions of a second after she was through with her accusations. From one moment to the next, the docile bore had disappeared, and a completely new man had taken his place. One who grabbed Penny roughly by the shoulders with both hands, shook her, and yelled at her.

His voice was that of a complete stranger. "You rotten little snoop," he yelled, "who do you think you are? Do you think I'm going to let you—?"

He didn't get any further, because at that moment the compartment door flew open and Inspector Moser rushed in. Much to Penny's relief, she had to admit. She had not been prepared for Martin to attack her physically.

Before Martin could get another word out, the young cop had already yanked him away from Penny and pushed him chest-first against the wall.

With a few swift moves that seemed practiced a hundred times over, Jürgen fixed Martin's arm in his back and incapacitated him. The next moment he eyed Penny with a concerned sideways glance.

"Are you all right?"

She nodded reluctantly.

Martin transformed back into a submissive sneak just as quickly as he had mutated into a berserker right before.

"You're hurting me," he groaned, but the inspector didn't let up. Instead, he gave Penny another look, this time a questioning one that could mean only one thing: "Did he confess to the murders?"

Penny shook her head. "Can I talk to you outside?" She urgently needed to share her new insight with Jürgen.

The inspector hesitated for a moment, but then let go of Martin Salmann, who fled as quickly as he could to the other side of the cabin. He dropped onto the sofa, and stared at Penny. There was still distaste in his eyes, but no trace of that spiteful rage which had just burst out of the otherwise unobtrusive man.

"You stay here and keep quiet," Jürgen ordered him. Whereupon Martin nodded submissively.

Penny turned away and stepped out into the aisle. The inspector followed her.

26

They walked down the aisle to the end of the car, then the police officer confronted Penny.

"I told you this was madness!" he snapped at her, but there was more concern than anger in his voice. "Luckily I just happened to be nearby and heard the guy yelling. Who knows what he would have done to you otherwise."

"I think he just blew a fuse," Penny said. She strongly suspected that the inspector had *happened to be near-by* the whole time. Presumably he had not followed her suggestion to search the rear cars for evidence, and had instead stood by to assist her in case of emergency.

Which Penny found very romantic, even if she had no intention of admitting it to herself.

"I threw some nasty accusations at Martin," she added quickly, trying not to blush with embarrassment. "And in the process, I probably put my finger in one wound or another."

Jürgen Moser looked at her mutely, and for a few moments a meaningful silence fell between them.

"I had an epiphany," Penny finally broke the silence. "Earlier, when Martin came at me. I had just accused him of killing his brothers and his mother in order to get his hands on the company."

Jürgen nodded, but didn't seem to be really listening to her. There was something in his eyes that had nothing to do with the murder case. In his very beautiful, deep eyes, as Penny noticed not for the first time.

She forced herself to ignore his gaze. Just like the warm feeling that was spreading through her own chest. No more flirting, she had a murder case to solve! She had finally stumbled onto something tangible that would get her somewhere. Hopefully.

"What if we were looking at the murders in the wrong order?" she said to Jürgen, emphasizing each word to give the question the necessary weight.

The inspector blinked. Then he rubbed his chin with his right hand, and the glimmer in his eyes went out. In the formal voice of the policeman he asked, "What are you getting at? The order of the murders is completely obvious, isn't it? First Xavier was killed, then Jacques, and then the mother—because she knew too much. At least that's what you told me. Is there anything wrong with that?"

"No... That is, yes."

Jürgen looked at her in confusion.

"I mean, of course they died in that order. There's no question about that. But what if Madeleine wasn't murdered because she saw something? What if we're just supposed to believe that, and she really wasn't an accidental witness to the crimes at all?"

"But?" asked Jürgen.

"But the actual victim! The most important one. Looking at it this way sheds a whole new light on the matter. I can't really find a valid reason why any of our four suspects would want to kill the two brothers. With Madeleine, on the other hand, the motive would be obvious."

The inspector shook his head. "It's sort of like that story where a man loses his house keys in the street at night and then looks for them in the light of the street lamp. Not because he lost them in that exact spot, but because it's bright there and he can see better. You can't make Madeleine the main victim just because a motive can be found for her murder."

"Don't you get it?" Penny blurted out. "Maybe that was exactly the killer's strategy! An ingenious cover-up tactic. He deliberately killed Madeleine at the end and made it look as if he had merely silenced a witness with this act. So we focused on the other two murders that were committed first—and would never have come up with the right motive."

"And where there is no motive, there is no connection to the murderer," Jürgen said slowly. At last he seemed to understand.

Penny nodded. "The killer made a mistake by killing Madeleine with the steak knife from the restaurant. That's been bothering me all night. As we've established, he couldn't have obtained that weapon on the spur of the moment, just before the crime."

"Which means the murder of Madeleine was planned some time before that," Jürgen completed her train of thought.

"Exactly. That is the only logical explanation. Somehow it was clear to me, but all night long I didn't understand what it really meant. It wasn't until just now, when Martin came at me, that I suddenly saw it very clearly in front of me."

"An epiphany at the moment of danger? Female intuition?" Jürgen's upper lip was twitching treacherously. Was he making fun of her?

"Call it what you like," she said, "I think I came up with it when I realized that tonight's three murders made Martin the sole heir to Madeleine's business. If you look at them as three *planned* murders, that's obvious—not two planned crimes plus the seemingly spontaneous elimination of a witness."

Jürgen raised no further objections, and so she continued: "Madeleine's company; that was the motive! She had to die because she wanted to sell the firm—instead of making Martin her successor. Her corporation is worth billions, and running it may well be the lifelong dream of a very ambitious person. That's understandable, isn't it? Anyone who owns such a company has it made, is respected and admired, and can realize their wildest dreams."

"And the two brothers?" interjected Jürgen, "why were they both murdered? I hope you're not saying it was just to cover up their mother's murder?"

"No, they had to die too, but they were just minor characters, not the main targets of the killer. The two were also in favor of selling the company. So, it wasn't enough to kill the mother, because after her death, Xavier and Jacques would have voted two to one against Martin, and the company would have been sold after all."

"So Martin is our culprit?"

Penny didn't answer right away.

"Hmm," she said then, "until half an hour ago, I wouldn't have thought he had any aggressive potential. But I was clearly wrong about that."

Jürgen grumbled something incomprehensible. It was obvious that in retrospect he did not approve of the risky interrogation that Penny had undertaken on her own. Neither as a policeman nor as a man.

"This crime is much more complex than it first appeared," Penny continued. "I can see that now. Let's summarize where we stand: if I'm right, Madeleine's murder was planned from the beginning, and the sequence was deliberately turned upside down to disguise the motive. The poisonous spider we were hunting never existed. The supposed spider bites were inflicted upon Xavier and Jacques with the help of a mini robot. Right under our noses. It took a good amount of intelligence and technical understanding to commit those murders. And plenty of risk-taking, especially when it came to killing Madeleine. The window of opportunity for that was tiny and the risk of being discovered was extremely high."

"And you don't grant Martin Salmann quite that much ingenuity," the inspector said. It was more a statement than a question.

Penny raised her shoulders. "Do you?" she replied.

"I've hardly had a chance to get a closer look at him. But judging by your descriptions, not really. While he's clearly not in control of himself, considering the way he went after you earlier, the murders were not committed in the heat of the moment. That much is certain."

"Right. And there's something else: if Martin had run to his mother's compartment to murder her, within the short period of time Schneiders was with me, he should have met his wife there."

"Then I guess Erika is our murderer after all?" the inspector asked.

"I have a certain suspicion," Penny said slowly. "But not a shred of evidence to back it up. I think we need to do a little experiment—if you don't mind."

Jürgen was immediately on his guard. "What kind of experiment?" he asked suspiciously.

"I'd like to have another conversation with Christiane Schneiders."

"The secretary?"

"Yes. But this time in your presence."

Jürgen shook his head vigorously. "We've already discussed that, haven't we? That's out of the question.

It could put me—"

"Yeah, all right," Penny interrupted him. "It could cost you your job. But if my experiment succeeds, you'll be able to present your superiors with a solved case. And arrest one hell of a clever murderer. Wouldn't that be something?"

27

Jürgen Moser followed Penny into the front car, to the secretary's compartment. He didn't let on what chaos reigned in his head; what kind of thoughts raged through his mind.

What on earth was he doing here? This woman, Penny, had him completely wrapped around her little finger; that much was obvious. He should never have gone along with her suggestion to question the suspects alone. To have this so-called *informal chat among civilians,* as she had put it in her inimitable way.

Fortunately, he had stayed close by earlier, instead of following her proposal and inspecting the rear cars of the train. This woman could not be left alone. She was too brave for her own good. Too adventurous, too crazy.

And now he was about to jeopardize his career for her. Of course, she hadn't told him a word about the experiment she was planning. And also, he wanted to solve the case. A few laurels, some praise from his superiors—that would unquestionably do his young career good. But for that reason alone he would never have agreed to Penny's request. To her mysterious experiment that was supposed to unmask the killer.

He felt the service weapon on his belt. He had to be on guard, to protect her, this redheaded whirlwind, if she maneuvered herself headlong into a life-threatening situation again, without even a thought of the possible risks.

What a woman. There was something strangely alluring about her, something that swept you along, whether you wanted it to or not. She reminded him of a great heroine of his childhood: Pippi Longstocking, the beloved book and movie character.

The flame-red hair. The freckles, even if they were only a few. The cheeky snub nose. The way Penny always seemed to know what to do, and how she took the initiative.

That was ridiculous, of course. He was no longer a little boy, but a grown man, a policeman, as he had always dreamed. And he had worked hard for it. The training had truly not been a piece of cake.

And yet this Penny was like Pippi: wild, impetuous, full of adventure, and completely headstrong. She didn't let anyone get her down, was seemingly fear-less. And she didn't care about any rules or regula-tions. You had to admire her. In secret, of course.

He smiled to himself as he followed her down the aisle. Determined, she headed for the secretary's cabin and, without knocking, opened the door.

The compartment was empty.

Penny turned and looked at him in irritation. "I

asked Schneiders to stay here," she said, sounding like a head teacher who couldn't believe her orders were being defied. Her snub nose twitched a little, and all at once she seemed nervous. She walked back a bit the way they had come, yanking open each compartment door.

They did not have to search for long. They found the secretary in the front compartment of the second carriage—where Jacques Salmann's fiancée and the doctor, Dr. Stiller, were also ensconced.

Schneiders was sitting next to Louise on the sofa and drinking tea. The two women seemed tired but calm, the doctor looking eager to serve—and clearly he had taken a liking to the grieving fiancée. Jürgen had an eye for that kind of thing.

Well, this Louise was also an exceptionally attractive woman. *But no comparison to Penny,* he told himself. And in the next moment he scolded himself for being a fool. He could not allow this woman to take over his thoughts.

He looked around the compartment attentively and then took up position right next to the door. With that, he stayed a few steps behind Penny, who marched blithely over to the sofa and came to a stop there in front of those present. Like a prosecutor in a courtroom.

She turned to Jacques Salmann's fiancée and said in a measured tone: "The case is solved. Martin Salmann killed your fiancé. Along with his other brother and his own mother."

Louise's mouth dropped open. She sought the doctor's gaze, while he protectively placed his hand on her arm. Then she burst into tears.

"But... why," she stammered, "why did he do that?"

The secretary, who was sitting next to Louise on the sofa, put down her teacup with a loud clink. She looked no less startled, but had a far better grip on herself than Jacques's widowed bride.

"I'll never believe it," she said in a sharp tone to Penny. "You must be mistaken. Mr. Salmann is most definitely not a murderer."

"I wouldn't have believed it either, but it's still true," Penny replied.

Schneiders pinched her lips. "I tell you, you are mistaken! The relationship between Martin and his brothers was not the very best, but what reason should he have had to murder them?"

"Oh, the murders weren't about the two brothers in the first place," Penny said lightly. As if she were merely reminding her listeners of the obvious.

"But?" asked Louise, sniffling.

Jürgen took a step forward to get a better view of everything. He didn't want to miss any details and forced himself to intently study the facial expressions of the two women on the sofa. In the past, he had not paid much attention to such things, but because of his police training he knew how important it was to be able to read human body language correctly.

But what was Penny getting at with her statement? Earlier, during their conversation in the corridor, she had expressed doubts as to whether Martin Salmann was really the perpetrator. And now she claimed it with conviction?

"The real victim was Madeleine," Penny said, turning back to Schneiders and seemingly ignoring Louise. "And Martin Salmann has confessed to the crime."

Even from his distance, Jürgen could see the secretary's pupils dilate at these words.

Confessed? What the heck was Penny talking about?

She gave him a quick glance over her shoulder that Jürgen couldn't interpret, then she continued—again addressing the assistant, "He made a full confession, but you're probably right, Schneiders. I don't think he's really our killer either. I'm pretty sure he's protecting his wife."

"His wife?" echoed Schneiders. Her pupils grew a little larger still.

Penny nodded. "Yes. In fact, barely half an hour before his confession, I happened to watch him pull her into his arms and profess his unconditional love for her. Not very polite of me to spy on the two of them, but the compartment door was ajar, and I just couldn't bring myself to ignore that invitation. I'm afraid I'm a terribly nosy woman."

She shrugged her shoulders. Then she continued, "Anyway. Martin promised his wife that everything would be all right, that he would protect her, come what may. Unbelievable that something like this still exists nowadays, don't you think? Such unconditional love that you're even willing to take up a life sentence for your wife." She let out a sigh, seemingly deeply touched, although Jürgen was pretty sure she was just putting on an act.

Louise snuggled against the doctor's shoulder, who was only too happy to offer her comfort; Schneiders, on the other hand, sat stock-still and looked like a pillar of salt.

Penny continued to talk, still in what appeared to be a light conversational tone, "I think in the end, though, Erika will be convicted. Using a poisonous spider as a murder weapon was a mistake. Martin doesn't know anything about these critters, but Erika does, as it turns out."

A deep wrinkle appeared on the secretary's forehead. She seemed to be thinking hard about Penny's words. Then, after a few seconds had passed, she began, "You know, maybe Mr. Salmann didn't confess out of love after all. Maybe he did—" She hesitated.

"Yeah?" encouraged Penny.

"Maybe he *did* commit the murders himself. I've been wondering all evening if the spider was really a spider."

"I'm afraid I don't follow you," Penny said. Which was a lie, as Jürgen knew, because they had both long since rejected the spider hypothesis as well.

Schneiders stood up, as if driven by a sudden impulse to stretch her feet a bit, and began to walk up and down the cabin. As she did so, she seemed deeply lost in thought.

28

"Do you have a better idea how the murders might have been committed?" Penny turned to the secretary. Jürgen still didn't have the slightest clue what kind of game she was actually playing.

"Possibly," Schneiders said. "I can't imagine how the killer would have used a live poisonous animal with such pinpoint accuracy. I think he used one of our company's products instead." She pointed to the robo-steward parked in a corner of the compartment. Jürgen hadn't noticed the little machine until now.

"We also create much smaller robots," the secretary said. "All the way down into the nano range. That's a big trend in the weapons industry, you know. Remote-controlled or even autonomous combat robots. And that's coupled with miniaturization. Mechanical soldiers that have no life to lose, need no sleep—and in the case of micro and nano robots, are also so small as to be as good as invisible. Perhaps Martin used such a weapon instead of a poisonous spider. The need for adaptation would certainly have been minimal."

Penny exclaimed in astonishment, then asked Schneiders all the questions that Jürgen had answered for her long ago. What did nano mean? How small could the combat robots actually get? How could they move and act autonomously? And so on.

The assistant readily provided information, in much more detail than Jürgen had been able to.

"Your technical know-how is really impressive, Schneiders, I'll give you that," Penny said at the end. "When all you were was Madame Salmann's assistant. Your boss should have made you at least a department head—then she might still be alive now. "

With these words, Penny suddenly turned to Jürgen and smiled triumphantly at him.

"Here you go," she announced in quite a stagy tone. "Now we have motive, opportunity, *and* also the necessary technical know-how, all combined in Ms. Schneiders. May I introduce you: here's our killer."

The secretary jerked her head up and stared at Penny in disbelief. Then she laughed throatily. "Very original indeed, Miss Küfer, but I'm afraid I can't find it funny."

"Oh, I'm not kidding," Penny returned, now in a very serious voice. "You're the only one aboard this train who meets all the requirements for being the killer. It took me way too long to realize that, but, well, better late than never. You know a lot about your company's combat robots. You adapted one of those mini-machines so it could fake a spider bite. You also had the opportunity to kill Madeleine. The story that she wanted to see me because she suspected or saw something was fictional. You grabbed a knife in the restaurant earlier that evening, and you used it to murder your boss *before* you came to my compartment. You also called Erika from Madeleine's phone and immediately hung up. That's how you lured her into Madeleine's compartment and thus to the scene of the crime and drew suspicion to her. Very cleverly set up, I'll give you that."

"You're out of your mind," the secretary hissed.

"That was an important part of your plan," Penny continued, seemingly unmoved. "That suspicion would fall on Martin's wife. That's why you came up with the poison spider idea; because you knew that Erika's first husband had died from a spider bite. Erika assured me that no one within the family knew about that incident, and Martin assured me the same. He, however, was lying. He had told someone about Erika's past, someone he trusted unconditionally: his mistress. And that's you, Schneiders."

Jürgen could not believe his ears. Martin Salmann and the assistant? He would never have thought of that. Well, at second glance, this Schneiders was quite an attractive woman, even if she dressed soberly and very strictly. And Erika Salmann was not exactly a fairytale princess either. Not to mention Martin himself.

Penny kept talking, not giving Schneiders time for further indignant interjections: "I'm sure Martin will confirm that he told you about Erika's past. And that you are his mistress."

"What nonsense," the assistant exclaimed. "He confessed to the murders, didn't he? He's the perpetrator!"

Penny waved it off. "I just made that up to throw you off your guard a little. I figured if I claimed he confessed to the crime out of love for his wife, you'd probably hate him for it—and want revenge right then and there. Kind as I am, I gave you the opportunity to get even immediately."

Pippi, no, *Penny*, crossed her arms in front of her chest. "And you jumped at the chance. At the beginning you tried to defend Martin. You really threw yourself into convincing me of his innocence. First, because you love him, and second, because it was exactly according to your plan to frame his wife for the murders. But then, when I invented the love scene between him and Erika, you changed your mind. From one second to the next. You felt betrayed by him, didn't you? You obviously hated him for loving his wife after all, even to the point of wanting to take a life sentence for her. And you realized that your ingenious murder plan had failed."

"What nonsense!" cried Schneiders. Her face was contorted into a hateful grimace.

But Penny continued to speak. Faster and faster the words came out of her mouth. "You wanted to take revenge on him now by doing everything you could to frame him for the crime. *Your crime*. Suddenly you claimed it was possible that he had committed the murders after all. Yes, you even kindly helped me by explaining how he must have done it. By using one of your company's diabolical miniature robots. It's a pity that, by doing so, you have demonstrated your own knowledge in this field. But tell me, Schneiders, what did Martin promise you when you became his mistress? That he would divorce Erika? And marry you?"

This time Schneiders remained silent, but Jürgen could tell by looking at her that Penny had hit the mark. Her lips quivered; her cheeks were red with anger. Human body language really was a fine thing.

"The charade you played for all of us tonight was really successful," Penny continued, not taking her eyes off the assistant. "A stage-worthy play. So perfectly orchestrated that you fooled us all, right from the start. The reversed order of the murders, first the brothers, then the mother, who apparently only died because she was a troublesome witness. The supposed spider bites, the pillbox with the hole in it that you smuggled into Erika's handbag—and on top of that the seemingly surprised look you gave your rival at dinner. Combined with the later claim that she had pulled a pillbox out of her purse—which, of course, wasn't the case, because Erika didn't know anything about this box. Maybe you even smuggled it into her purse much later. In any case, I naïvely went along with this game and inquired about that strange glance you shot Erika at dinner. Which gave you the opportunity to cast suspicion on her—your hated rival."

29

"You're not half as smart as you think you are, Miss Küfer," Schneiders snarled. Her mouth was a hard line now, and Jürgen noticed her squinting several times toward the compartment door. But she didn't stand a chance; she wouldn't get past him if she tried to escape.

"Maybe I'm not as smart as you, Schneiders," Penny shot back, "but unlike you, I'm not a psychopath who ruthlessly murders people just to achieve their goals."

"What kind of goals?" Jürgen chimed in. He had actually intended to let Penny do her thing undisturbed, her so-called little experiment, which he still didn't fully understand.

But now he could stand it no longer. He finally had to know why she had suddenly accused Schneiders of the murders, acting so confidently, as if she didn't have the slightest doubt about the secretary's guilt. Or was it just an act to get Schneiders to confess?

Jürgen could see Penny stepping from one foot to the other, a moment of uncertainty, but in the next she was already Pippi Longstocking again, his heroine who didn't let anything get her down.

She briefly glanced at him and gave him a warm, if

rather nervous, smile. "The goals Schneiders was pursuing were superbly ambitious," she explained to him, with a sideways glance at the assistant. "She wanted it all at once: to have Martin for herself and to take control of Madeleine's company."

"The company?" This interjection came from Dr. Stiller, who was probably going through a similar experience as Jürgen himself. He certainly couldn't believe his ears either, at what seemingly crazy claims Penny was making.

Jürgen agreed with the doctor. "Why should a secretary lust after her boss's company? After all, I let myself believe that she wanted Martin for herself, and possibly his inheritance. Madeleine was an old lady who would have died a natural death in the not-too-distant future, and Martin had the prospect of a huge fortune, even if he had to share it with his brothers."

"I am not and never have been this man's mistress!" Schneiders insisted. "I resent this slander!"

"She wasn't in it for the money," Penny said, ignoring the interjection. "That is, not only. I think she wanted much more. She wanted to be at the top of one of the most visionary companies in the world. She longed for a position befitting her intellectual gifts and diligence. At least in her own eyes. Unfortunately, her boss didn't see it that way."

She turned to Schneiders. "Let me try to put myself in your shoes. You are a highly intelligent woman, with excellent technical expertise, and have been

Madeleine's assistant for many years. Practically around the clock. And how did she repay you? She treated you almost like a serf, didn't she? Instead of recognizing that you felt destined for much greater things. I have to rely on conjecture here, but surely you tried at one time or another to make a career for yourself, to get Madeleine to give you a department or something similar. But she wouldn't hear of it—either because she didn't see your talent, or out of entirely selfish motives—because she didn't want to lose her extremely capable assistant. And then you fell in love with Martin; perhaps because, like you, he was always in Madeleine's shadow?"

Schneiders kept a straight face.

"Well, anyway," Penny went on, "suddenly you saw a chance to get to the top, even take over the company yourself, by marrying Martin and getting his mother out of the way. He would legally be the company owner, but would surely be only too happy to let you take over once you were his wife. Martin has neither great professional vision nor the gumption to run a technological powerhouse. You, on the other hand, obviously felt quite confident about such a prospect. Even craved it. Only a few troublesome family members stood in the way of your ambitions."

"Do I have to listen to this?" Schneiders turned to Jürgen. "That's slander! Who does this woman think she is, acting the great prosecutor here?"

Jürgen knew only too well that the latter question

was justified. But now there was no turning back. He only prayed, by all that was sacred to him, that Penny was not mistaken. That she knew what she was doing. That Schneiders really was guilty in the end, and that it could be proven. Otherwise... No, he preferred not to think about that.

"Go ahead, Miss Küfer," he said to Penny in a formal tone, rather than addressing Schneiders' complaint.

Penny did not need to be told twice. Again, she put the assistant through the wringer and continued her accusation: "You made only a few mistakes in your ingenious plan. Perhaps the biggest was that you underestimated Erika. You see, she found out that her husband was having an affair, within his company, even though she didn't know that *you* were his mistress. With this piece of the puzzle that Erika provided me, suddenly everything made sense. You were the only female company employee among the murder suspects. And it was suddenly clear to me why Erika should be charged with the crimes. If she had been convicted as a murderer, Martin would certainly have divorced her. And the path would have been cleared for you. Therefore, instead of simply staging three accidents, you faked only two and then added an unequivocal murder. You couldn't very well have framed Erika for mere accidents. Really bold, I must say: three birds with one stone. The company owner who wanted to sell the business is out of the way, as are the two brothers who were also in favor of the sale and would never have given Martin sole management of the company. And Martin would divorce his wife and marry you instead. That was your plan, wasn't it?"

Schneiders gave no answer. Now that she had probably realized she could not expect any support from Jürgen, she stared out of the car window into the impenetrable snowy desert, seemingly bored.

"But you made another mistake," Penny continued. "I have been wondering all night why the murderer killed Madeleine with a knife instead of bringing his spider to bear a third time. In doing so, he outed himself as a murderer, whereas we had previously assumed tragic accidents involving a venomous spider. At first, I thought he had already disposed of the spider after the first two murders. But at the same time, I realized that he must have also obtained the knife hours earlier. The only possible conclusion was that he *wanted* his actions to look like murder. And what was the point of all this? I could think of no other explanation than that he was trying to frame someone. Namely Erika; because the spider poison clearly pointed to her, and she had also been lured to the crime scene by a fake phone call. The only question left was who would benefit from Erika's arrest. The answer? Martin's lover—you. Sound logic, isn't it? And you certainly excel at logic, I suppose."

Penny stepped right in front of Schneiders, putting her hands on the hips. "Give up," she said, "Martin won't marry you. He'll believe my arguments. And

Major Crimes will, too. You can forget about getting your hands on Madeleine's business."

Schneiders stood motionless for a moment. Her lips quivered; a vein throbbed on her forehead.

Then she said something very strange. "George, evacuation." And with that, the lights went out in the compartment.

In the sudden darkness, Jürgen was as good as blind. He couldn't see what happened next, he only heard a soft mechanical whir followed by rapid footsteps coming towards him. No, they were heading for the door!

Quickly he turned in the same direction, but then suddenly Penny cried out, and the next instant something hard rammed into him at knee level. The darn robo-steward! It was from him that the whirring had emanated. Schneiders had made the little tin guy her accomplice.

Jürgen buckled, went down, and could only dimly make out a shadow scurrying past him toward the door, which was torn open and immediately slammed shut again. Schneiders! She was trying to escape.

He had to stop her, no matter what. A nasty pain was throbbing in his knee, but he forced himself to his feet, limping toward the exit he could now slowly make out. His eyes, fortunately, were adjusting quickly to the darkness. He stumbled out into the corridor, at the end of which Schneiders' shadowy figure was already reaching the airlock between the train cars.

A hiss followed.

The outer doors, was all Jürgen could think. The murderess had managed to unlock them. Just as she seemed to have the entire technology of the train under her control, starting with the lighting and the cursed robot that had rammed him. Dash it!

As fast as his feet would carry him, Jürgen ran along the corridor. His knee already felt like a dull mass consisting of nothing but pain. But he couldn't let Schneiders get away; with no visibility in the blizzard out there, she could vanish into thin air within a few feet, never to be seen again—apart from the fact that they would both inevitably freeze to death in a chase.

30

Penny gratefully reached for the hot cup of tea the steward handed her. The steward from the lounge car, a human being made of flesh and blood. She had had enough of robots for now.

She was standing in the corridor in front of Schneiders's cabin—which Jürgen had unceremoniously converted into Schneiders's cell.

Penny had been in great fear for the brave inspector when she had seen him hobble off the train behind the murderess, out into the icy wasteland where the blizzard still raged. She had followed them, a few feet behind, after recovering from the blow George had dealt her. What a name for a robot! And what an efficient battering ram the little guy had been. Penny's shin still hurt like hell. But still, the joy—no, the triumphant feeling—that everything was finally over outweighed any pain.

All her finesse and technical know-how had been of no use to Schneiders in the end. Jürgen had caught up with her, outside on the platform, before she could dissolve into the swirling white of the storm. The fight between the two had not lasted long. Physically, Schneiders was inferior in every respect to the well-

trained young inspector. Finally he had dragged her back onto the train in handcuffs and had locked her safely in her own cabin.

During the subsequent questioning, the murderer finally confessed. This time it was the inspector who'd conducted the interrogation, although Penny, of course, had not missed the opportunity to eavesdrop through the door. By a strange coincidence, it had stood slightly ajar.

Schneiders did not seem to feel the slightest remorse for her actions, but described to the inspector every single step of her plan, down to the last gruesome detail. There was unmistakable pride in her voice.

Penny essentially learned nothing more that she didn't already know or at least had suspected. Although in the end the murderer had almost managed to escape responsibility for her crimes with the help of George.

Schneiders had reprogrammed the robo-steward, who outwardly resembled his more harmless colleagues down to the last screw, for her purposes. At her command, the mechanical accomplice had made the lights go out and unlocked the outer doors, all wirelessly, of course, as was common these days. And he had also proved to be quite a useful weapon, as Penny and Jürgen were able to attest.

But Schneiders had long since disposed of her secret weapon, the much smaller robot, which, according to her claim, had actually been only as big as an ant. She had crushed it to scrap under her shoe heel and then dumped the individual parts in the toilet. When asked how she had gotten the spider venom, she'd merely shrugged and said, "Internet shopping."

Much later, when Major Crimes had finally arrived and taken over the case, Penny stood in the corridor with Jürgen Moser for the last time. With *her* inspector, as she had come to call him. Only in her thoughts, of course.

The time for saying goodbye had come. Penny could hardly keep her eyes open. She was cold, hungry and dead tired. But it was done. The murder on the Occident Express had been solved. The killer had been brought to justice.

"Awesome teamwork," she said to Jürgen and gave him a smile. He really was an attractive man. Who knows, maybe she would meet him again someday.

St. Anton wasn't the end of the world, after all. And she was single now.

He returned her smile with a mischievous grin. "You're amazing, Penny," he said. "I don't even dare imagine the cases you'll solve once you're done with your detective training."

Her training. She knew now that she had made the right decision, even if the price had been exceedingly high. Her professional dream had cost her her engagement, her inheritance, and her relationship with her mother, even if that relationship had never been the best. But after this night, Penny knew one thing with one hundred percent certainty: she wanted nothing more in the world than to become a real detective.

Enjoyed the book?

Please consider leaving a star rating or a short review on Amazon. Thank you!

More from Penny Küfer?

DEATH OF A SNOOP
Penny Küfer investigates, Book 2

Instead of cramming for her degree at the detective academy, Penny Küfer, aspiring sleuth, finds herself in a "lost place", a former grand hotel near the magic mountain of Semmering. Recently a particularly devious murderer seems to have checked in, plus there is a strange rumor about a secret hiding place full of diamonds...

About the author

Alex Wagner lives with her husband near Vienna, Austria. From her writing chair she has a view of an old castle ruin, which helps her to dream up the most devious murder plots.

Alex writes murder mysteries set in the most beautiful locations of Europe and in popular holiday spots. If you love to read Agatha Christie and other authors from the "Golden Age" of mystery fiction, you will enjoy her stories.

You can learn more about her and her books on the internet and on Facebook:

www.alexwagner.at
www.facebook.com/AlexWagnerMysteryWriter

Printed in Great Britain
by Amazon